...dare.

But she'd have to. Tonight's success rested on her being one hundred and ten per cent on her game. Her mother had taught her well—go easy on the alcohol or make a fool of herself. Not going to happen tonight, when everyone's eyes would be on her.

Zac's throat worked as he tasted the champagne. Appreciation lit up his eyes. His tongue licked his bottom lip.

And Olivia melted: deep inside where she'd stored all her Zac memories there was a pool of hot, simmering need. The glass clinked against her teeth as the divine liquid spilled across her tongue. And while her shoulders lightened, tension of a different kind wound into a ball in her tummy and down to her core.

'Delicious,' she whispered.

Zac or the wine?

Dear Reader,

Fiji is one of the world's treasures, with lots of beautiful islands where resorts sit beneath the palms, surrounded by the bluest of seas where the most colourful fish live. Kayaking around the islands is an adventure like none I've experienced elsewhere.

When I was thinking about this story the idea of sending Olivia and Zac there while they got to know each other just popped into my head—and so here they are. These two have had a strong physical relationship in the past, but this time they need to get to know each other far better—and where better than on a tiny island in the middle of the ocean?

Zac and Olivia both need to learn to trust their instincts and follow their hearts. Of course it's not easy, but the end result will be worth it. I love giving my characters their happy-ever-after. I hope you enjoy this one.

I'd love to hear from you on sue.mackay56@yahoo.com, or drop by suemackay.co.nz.

All the best,

Sue

BREAKING
ALL THEIR RULES

BY
SUE MacKAY

MILLS
BOON

Published in Great Britain 2016
By Mills & Boon, an imprint of HarperCollins*Publishers*
1 London Bridge Street, London, SE1 9GF

© 2016 Sue MacKay

ISBN: 978-0-263-25436-5

Our policy is to use papers that are natural, renewable and recyclable
products and made from wood grown in sustainable forests. The logging
and manufacturing processes conform to the legal environmental
regulations of the country of origin.

Printed and bound in Spain
by CPI, Barcelona

Sue MacKay lives with her husband in New Zealand's beautiful Marlborough Sounds, with the water at her doorstep and the birds and the trees at her back door. It is the perfect setting to indulge her passions of entertaining friends by cooking them sumptuous meals, drinking fabulous wine, going for hill walks or kayaking around the bay—and, of course, writing stories.

Books by Sue MacKay

Mills & Boon Medical Romance

Doctors to Daddies
A Father for Her Baby
The Midwife's Son

Surgeon in a Wedding Dress
The Dangers of Dating Your Boss
Every Boy's Dream Dad
Christmas with Dr Delicious
You, Me and a Family
The Gift of a Child
From Duty to Daddy
A Family This Christmas
The Family She Needs
Midwife...to Mum!
Reunited...in Paris!
A December to Remember

Visit the Author Profile page
at millsandboon.co.uk for more titles.

Dear Lyn, I am going to miss your laugh
and those good times we yakked in your sewing room.
Thank you for dragging me out to find my other passions
that I'd forgotten all about until I met you. You read
every book and this one is definitely for you.

CHAPTER ONE

OLIVIA COATES-CLARK STRAIGHTENED up and indicated to a nurse to wipe her forehead in an attempt to get rid of an annoying tickle that had been irritating her for some minutes. 'Is it me, or is Theatre hotter than usual this morning?'

'I haven't noticed,' Kay, the anaesthetist, answered as she kept an eye on the monitors in front of her. 'Sure you're not stressing about tonight, Olivia?'

'Me? Stress?' Olivia grimaced behind her mask. She was a control freak; of course she stressed. 'Okay, let's get this second implant inserted so we can bring our girl round.'

'So everything's good to go for the gala fundraiser?' Kay persisted.

'Fingers crossed,' Olivia muttered, refusing to think about what could go wrong. Her list of requirements and tasks was complete, neat little ticks beside every job and supplier and by the name of every attendee, including the seeing eye dog coming.

'I bumped into Zac yesterday. He's looking forward to catching up with everyone.' Kay's forced nonchalance didn't fool her.

'I'm sure everyone feels the same.' The anaesthetist *had* hit on the reason for Olivia feeling unnaturally hot. Zachary Wright. Just knowing he'd be at the function she'd spent weeks organising made her toes curl with unwanted anticipation. Not to mention the alien nervousness. 'Zac,' she sighed into her mask. The one man she'd never been able to delete from her mind. And, boy, had she tried.

'You need more mopping?' the nurse asked.

'No, thanks.' That particular irritation had gone, and she'd ignore the other—Zac—by concentrating on supervising the plastic surgery registrar opposite her as he placed the tissue expander beneath the pocket under Anna Seddon's pectoralis major muscle on the left side of her chest wall.

The registrar had supported Olivia as she'd done the first insertion of an expander on the right side, watching every move she made, listening to every word she said, as though his life depended on it. Which it did. One mistake and she'd be on him like a ton of bricks. So far he was doing an excellent job of the second breast implant. 'Remember to make sure this one's placed exactly the same as the first one. No woman is going to thank you for lopsided breasts.' This might only be the first stage in a series of surgeries to reconstruct Anna's breasts but it had to be done well. There was no other way.

The guy didn't look up as he said, 'I get it. This is as much about appearances and confidence as preventing cancer.'

'Making a person feel better about themselves is our job description.' Her career had evolved along a path of repairing people who'd had misadventures or deforming surgeries. But she didn't knock those specialists working to make people happier in less traumatic circumstances. Everyone was entitled to feel good about themselves, for whatever reasons; to hide behind a perfect facade if they needed to.

For Olivia, looking her absolute best was imperative: a confident shield that hid the messy, messed-up teenager from the critical world waiting to pounce. Making the most of her appearance hadn't been about attracting males and friends since she was twelve and the night her father had left home for the last time, taking his clothes and car, and her heart. Leaving her to deal with her mother's problems alone.

Kay glanced down at the table. 'This isn't the first time I've seen a perfectly healthy woman deliberately have her breasts removed, but I still can't get my head round it. I don't know if I'd have the guts to have the procedure done if I didn't already have cancer.'

Olivia understood all too well, but... 'If you'd lost your grandmother and one sister to the disease, and your mother had had breast cancer you might think differently.' Bad luck came in all forms.

'I'd do whatever it took to be around to watch my kids grow up,' one of the nurses said.

'You're right, and so would I.' Kay shivered. 'Still, it's a huge decision. You'd want your man on side, for sure.'

'Anna's husband's been brilliant. I'd go so far as to call him a hero. He's backing her all the way.' A hero? If she wasn't in Theatre she'd have to ask herself what she was on. Heroes were found in romance stories, not real life—not often anyhow, and not in her real life. Not that she'd ever let one in if one was on offer.

As Olivia swabbed the incision a clear picture of Zac spilled into her mind, sent a tremor down her arm, had her imagining his scent. *Oh, get over yourself.* Zac wasn't her hero. Wasn't her *anything*. Hadn't been since she'd walked away from their affair eighteen months ago. But—she sighed again—what would've happened if she'd found the courage to push the affair beyond the sex and into a relationship where they talked and shared and had been there for each other? Eventually Zac would've left her. At least by getting in first she'd saved herself from being hurt. Tonight she'd see quite a bit of him, which didn't sit easily with her. The day his registration for the gala had arrived in her inbox she'd rung him for a donation for the fundraising auction. Since then she hadn't been able to erase him from her mind. *Come on. He's always been lurking in the back of your head, reminding you how good you were together.*

'So there are good guys out there.' Kay's tone was acerbic.

Zac might be one of the good guys. She hadn't hung round long enough to find out. She'd got too intense about him too quickly and pulling the plug on their fling had been all about staying in control and not setting herself up to be abandoned. Going through that at twelve had been bad enough; to happen again when she was an adult would be ridiculous. So she'd run. Cowardly for sure, but the only way to look out for herself. And now she had an op to finish and a gala to start. 'Let's get this tidied up and the saline started.' She had places to be and hopefully not many things to do.

An hour later she was beginning to wish she'd stayed in Theatre for the rest of the day. The number of texts on her phone gave the first warning that not everything was going to plan at the hotel where the gala evening would be held; that her list was in serious disarray.

As she ran for her car, the deluge that all but drowned her and destroyed her carefully styled hair, which she'd spent the evening before having coloured and tidied, was the second warning. At least her thick woollen coat had saved her silk blouse from ruin. But rain had not been on her schedule, which put her further out of sorts. *Everything* about tonight had to be perfect.

Slamming the car door, she glared out at the black sky through the wet windscreen. 'Get a move on. I want you gone before my show starts tonight.'

The third suggestion that things were turning belly up was immediate and infuriating. One turn of the ignition key and the flat clicking sound told a story of its own. The battery was kaput. Because? Olivia slapped the dashboard with her palm. The lights had been left on. There was no one to blame except herself.

Olivia knew the exact moment Zac walked through the entrance of the plush hotel, and it had nothing to do with the sudden change in noise as the doors opened, letting in sounds of rain and car horns. She might've been facing the receptionist but she knew. Her skin prickled, her belly tightened, and the air around her snapped. Worse, she forgot whatever it was she'd been talking about to the young woman on the other side of the polished oak counter.

So nothing had changed. He still rattled her chain, made her feel hot and sexy and out of control—and he hadn't even said a word to her. Probably hadn't recognised her back view.

'Hello, Olivia. It's been a while.'

That particular husky, sexy voice belonged to only one man. 'Since what, Zac?' she asked, as she lifted her head and turned to face him, fighting the adrenaline rush threatening to turn her into a blithering wreck. This was why she'd left him. Zac undermined her self-control. How had she found the strength to walk away? Not that there'd been anything more to their relationship than sex. Nothing that should be making her blood fizz and her heart dance a tango just because he stood a few feet from her. No way did she want to jump his bones within seconds of seeing him. She shouldn't want to at all. But no denying it—she did. Urgently.

Black-coffee-coloured eyes bored into her, jolting her deep inside. 'Since we last spent the night together, enjoying each other's company.'

'Go for the jugular, why don't you?' she gasped, knowing how wrong it was to even wish he'd give her a hug and say he'd missed her.

Zac instantly looked contrite. 'Sorry, Olivia. I didn't mean to upset you.'

'You didn't,' she lied. Behind her physical reaction her heart was sitting up, like it had something to say. Like what? Not going there. 'The bedroom scene was the grounds of our relationship.' That last night she'd got up at three in the morning, said she couldn't do it any more, and had walked out without explaining why. To tell him her fears would've meant exposing herself, and that was something she never did.

'So? How's things? Keeping busy?' Inane, safe, and so not what she really wanted to ask. *Got a new woman in your life? Do you ever miss me? Even a teeny, weeny bit? Or are you grateful I pulled the plug when I did?* Right now all her muscles felt like they were reaching for him, wanting him touching them, rubbing them, turning her on even more. Had she done the right thing in leaving? Of course she had. Rule number one: stay in control. She'd been losing it back then. Fast.

Zac had the audacity to laugh. 'What? You haven't kept tabs on me?' His grin was lazy, and wide, and cut into her with the sexiness of it. There was no animosity there whatsoever, just a deliberate, self-mocking gleam in his beautiful eyes. He was as good as her at hiding emotions.

Shaking her head at him, Olivia leaned back, her hands pressed against the counter at her sides, the designer-jeans-clad legs Zac had sworn were the best he'd ever had anything to do with posed so that one was in front of the other and bent slightly at the knee, tightening the already tight, annoyingly damp denim over her not-so-well-toned thigh. 'My turn to apologise. I haven't kept up with any gossip.'

'Dull as dishwater, that's my life.' Unfortunately that twinkle she'd always melted for was very apparent, belying his statement.

'Right.' She rolled her eyes at him, unable to imagine Zac not being involved in and with people, especially feminine, good-looking, sexy people. Was she jealous? Couldn't be. She'd done the dumping, not him. But Zac with another woman? Pain lodged in the region of her heart.

'Never could fool you.' It was inordinately satisfying to see his gaze drop to the line on the front of her thigh where the mulberry three-quarter-length coat cut across her jeans. Even more gratifying when his tongue lapped that grin, which rapidly started fading. And downright exciting to see Zachary blink not once but twice.

She didn't need exciting in her life right now, and Zac and exciting were one and the same. 'I keep to myself a lot these days too,' she muttered, not really sure what she was talking about any more with the distracting package standing right in front of her.

'Now I'm shocked.' The grin was back in place,

lion-like in its power to knock her off her feet and set her quaking.

'Why? It's not as though I've ever been a social butterfly.'

'There's never been anything butterfly-like about you, Olivia.'

Confidence oozed from Zac that didn't bode well for the coming evening when they'd be in the same crowd, the same venue. At the same table. Of all the things she'd organised she should've been able to arrange that he sat on the opposite side of the room. It had proved impossible as they were the only two people attending the gala who were on their own. All the others were in pairs.

'You're saying I'm not a flapper?' They were toying with each other. Reality slammed into her, made her gasp aloud. They'd teased each other mercilessly the first night they'd gone to bed together, and had never stopped. Well, she was stopping now. Time to put distance between them. She needed to get on with what she was supposed to be doing. 'I've got a lot to do so I'll see you later. I hope you have a great evening.'

Disappointment flicked through his eyes, quickly followed by something much like hurt but couldn't be. Not hurt. She hadn't done anything more than push him aside, though that'd probably spiked his pride. He had a reputation of loving and leaving.

It had taken the death of a small child in Theatre to throw them into each other's arms for the first time. Desperate to obliterate the anguished parents from her mind, Olivia had found temporary comfort with Zac. She'd also found sex like she'd never known before. How they'd spent years rubbing shoulders at med school and not felt anything for each other until that day was one of life's mysteries. From then on all it took had been one look and they'd be tearing each other's clothes off, falling into bed, onto the couch, over the table. They'd done little talking and a lot of action.

Tonight, if they were stuck together for any length of time, she'd talk and keep her hands to herself. That had been the plan, but so far it wasn't working out. Not that she'd touched Zac yet. Yet? With her mouth watering and her fingers twitching, it would take very little to change that. She had to get serious and focus on what had to be done. 'I'll leave you to check in.' Her voice was pitched high—definitely no control going on there.

'I'm not checking in.'

She should've remembered that. She knew all the names of the people who'd elected to stay the night here instead of driving home afterwards. 'Do you live nearby?'

'Over the road.'

'In that amazing apartment building designed to look like a cruise ship, overlooking the super yachts and high-end restaurants?' Oh, wow. He had done all right for himself. Of course, he came from a moneyed background, but she recalled him saying he'd paid his own way through med school. She had never told him she also came from money or that her mother had used it to bribe her to keep her onside until she was old enough to work out that hiding bottles of alcohol from her father wasn't a joke at all.

'Are you staying here?' he asked casually, making her wonder if he might have plans to pay her a visit if she was.

'Yes.' The house she'd bought last summer was less than twenty minutes away in upmarket Parnell. 'I'm going to be busy here right up to kick-off, and going home to get ready for the evening would use up time I might not have if things go wrong.' Which plenty had done already. She looked over at the receptionist, suddenly remembering she'd been in the middle of another conversation before Zac had walked up. 'Can you let me know when Dr Brookes and his family check in, please?'

The girl nodded. 'Certainly, Dr Coates-Clark.'

'I'll be in the banquet room,' Olivia told the girl needlessly. The hotel staff had her cell number, but right now she wasn't doing so well on remembering anything she should. Better get a grip before the evening got under way.

Zac shrugged those impressive shoulders that she'd kissed many times. 'I'll give you a hand.'

'Thanks, but that won't be necessary. I'm getting everything sorted.' As much as having someone to help her would be a benefit, Zac would probably get her into a bigger pickle just by being in the same room. Turning on her heel, Olivia headed to the elevator that'd take her up to the room where tonight's dinner, auction, and dance would be held. The evening was due to get under way in a little over three hours and she wanted to check that everything was in place and see if the flowers had finally arrived. Something about bad weather causing a shortage of flowers at the markets that morning had been the harried florist's excuse. But bad weather didn't explain why the place name cards were yet to arrive from the copy centre.

Unbelievable how she'd softened on the inside when she'd first looked at Zac, despite the heat and turmoil he instantly ramped up within her. Like she'd missed him. But she hadn't known Zac beyond work and bed so not a lot to miss apart from that mind-blowing sex.

Odd she felt there was more to him she wanted to learn about when she hadn't been interested before. Not interested? Of course she had been. That's what had frightened her into ending the affair.

A large palm pressed the button to summon the elevator. 'It's out there on the surgeons' loop that you need some help with running the auction tonight. I'm stepping up. Starting now.' Zac looked down his long straight nose at her, his mouth firm, his gaze determined. 'No argument.'

Why would he want to do that? It meant being in her company for hours. She'd have sworn he would've planned on keeping well away from her, and that the last five minutes had been five too many in her company. 'Thanks, but no thanks, Zac. I've got it covered.' Second lie in minutes. She doubted she could spend too much time with him without dredging up all the reasons why she'd been a fool to drop him—instead of remembering why it had been a very sane move. No one was going to walk away from her ever again.

She made the mistake of looking at Zac and her tongue instantly felt too big for her mouth. Zac was so good looking, his face a work of art, designed to send any female who came near him into a lather. Including her. Olivia closed her eyes briefly, but his face followed her, seared on the insides of her eyelids. Zachary Wright. If ever there was a man she might fall for, it was Zac. That was a big 'if'. Painful lessons growing up were a harsh reminder that there was only one person who'd look out for her—herself.

But one touch and Zac had always been able to do anything he liked with her. Not that he'd taken advantage in a bad way. He wasn't that kind of man. See? She did know something about him. Hopefully he hadn't known how close she'd come to being totally his, as in willing to do absolutely anything to keep him.

'You all right?' He touched her upper arm, and despite her layers of clothing the heat she associated with him shot through her, consumed her.

'F-fine,' was all Olivia could manage as she stared at him, pushing down hard on the urge to touch him back, to run her hand over his cheek, and to feel that stubble beginning to darken his chin.

Taking her elbow, Zac propelled her forward, into the elevator. 'Third floor?'

'Yes,' she croaked. *Go away, leave me alone, take your sexy body and those eyes that were always my undoing, and take a flying leap off a tall building. I don't need this heat and need crawling along my veins. Go away.*

'I'm not going anywhere for the rest of the day, so get used to the idea, Olivia.'

Ouch. Had she said that out loud? What else had she put out there? One glance at him and she relaxed. He hadn't heard anything about jumping off a building. But she couldn't relax fully until tonight was put to bed.

Olivia groaned. 'Bed' was so not a safe word when she was around this man. It brought all sorts of images screaming into her head. Images she refused to see or acknowledge. They were her past, not her future. Or her present.

CHAPTER TWO

WHO'S TAKEN ALL the air out of this box? Zac stared around the elevator car, looking for a culprit. His eyes latched onto Olivia. He had his answer. It was *her* fault he couldn't breathe, couldn't keep his heart beating in a normal, steady rhythm. Olivia Coates-Clark. CC for short. CC *was* short. Delicate looking—not delicate of mind. Tiny, yet big on personality. Filled out in all the right places—as he well knew. Fiery when pushed too far, sweet when everything was going her way. An itch.

An itch he would never scratch again. He absolutely had to ignore it.

She'd dumped *him*. Hard and fast. Slapped at his pride. *He* did the leaving, when he was good and ready, not the other way round. He should've been grateful, was grateful. Having more than his usual three or four dates with Olivia had got him starting to look out for her. On the rare unguarded moments when something like deep pain had crept into her gaze he'd wanted to protect her; and that was plain dumb. Given his past, that made him a danger to her. He hurt people; did not protect them. He also didn't feel like having his heart cut and cauterised again when she learned of his inadequacies. No, thanks.

Hang on. Had she found out? Was that why Olivia

had pulled the plug on their affair? Because she'd found him to be flawed? No. She still looked at him as she always had—hot and hungry, not disgusted or aloof.

Breathing was impossible. Not only was Olivia using up the oxygen, she was filling the resulting vacuum with the scent of flowers and fruit and everything he remembered about her. *Hell, let me out of this thing. Fast.* He took a step towards the doors, stopped, glanced at the control panel. They were moving between floors. *Get a hold of yourself.*

Yeah, sure. This is what Olivia always did to him. Tipped him upside down with a look, sent his brain to the dump with a finger touch, and cranked up his libido so fast and high just by being in the same air as him. Exactly what was happening now. His crotch was tight, achingly tight. As was his gut. Nothing new there. Eighteen months without setting eyes on her, with only once talking on the phone about the auction, and he was back to square one. Back to lusting after her. Unbelievable. How could a grown man with a successful career as an orthopaedic surgeon, presumably an intelligent and sane man dedicated to remaining uninvolved with women, lose all control because of this one?

Olivia Coates-Clark. She was why he felt three sheets to the wind—and he hadn't touched a drop of alcohol all week. He'd been too busy with scheduled surgeries and two emergencies involving major operations to have any time to enjoy a drink and take in the ever-changing view from his apartment living room. But within minutes of being with CC he felt as though he'd downed a whole bottle of whiskey. This was shaping up to be a big night in a way he didn't need.

A phone buzzed discreetly. As nothing vibrated on

his hip it had to be Olivia's. He listened with interest as she answered, totally unabashed about eavesdropping.

'Olivia Coates-Clark speaking.' Her gaze scanned the ceiling as she listened to her caller. Then, 'Thank you so much. Your efforts are really appreciated.' Her finger flicked across the screen and the phone was shoved back into her pocket. 'One problem sorted.' She smiled directly at him.

'Had a few?' he asked, trying to ignore the jolt of need banging into his groin as his gaze locked on those lush lips.

'I guess it would be too much to expect arranging something as big as this has become to go off without some hitches. It hasn't been too bad, though.' Had she just crossed her fingers?

'Whose idea was it to raise money for Andy Brookes? Yours?'

Olivia nodded, and her copper-blonde hair brushed her cheek, adding further to his physical discomfort. 'I'll put my hand up, but from the moment I started talking to surgeons at Auckland Surgical Hospital it went viral. Everyone wants to be a part of supporting Andy. I imagine tonight's going to raise a fair whack of dosh. People have been unbelievably generous with offering art, holidays, and other amazing things to auction.' She smiled again, her mouth curving softly, reminding him of how he used to like lying beside her in his bed, watching her as she dozed after sex. All sweet and cute, and vastly different from the tigress who could sex him into oblivion. 'Thank you for your generous gift,' she was saying.

He'd put in a weekend for a family of four on his luxury yacht, with all the bells and whistles, and he'd be at the helm. 'Andy was the most popular guy in our senior registrar years. He never failed to help someone out when they were down.'

'You forget the practical jokes.' Again she smiled, making those full lips impossible to ignore.

So he didn't; studied them instead. Covered in a deep pink sheen, he could almost feel them on his skin as she kissed his neck just below his ear, or touched his chest, his belly, his… He groaned inwardly and leaned away from her, concentrating on having a polite conversation with his ex-lover. 'I have vivid memories of some of the things Andy did to various people.' He sighed as he tried to ease his need. Memories. There were far too many of Olivia stacked up in his mind. He should've heeded them and replied no to the invitation to join his colleagues tonight. He could've said he was doing the laundry or cleaning his car. But he'd wanted—make that needed—to get her out of his system once and for all, and had thought joining her tonight would be the ticket. Now he'd like nothing more than the gala to be over so he could head across the road to his quiet, cold apartment and forget Olivia.

'Have you met Andy's wife?'

'Kitty was at a conference with Andy that we attended in Christchurch last year.' *The conference you were supposed to speak at and cancelled the day after you walked out of my life.*

Olivia must've recalled that too because a shadow fell over those big eyes, darkening the hyacinth blue shade to the colour of ashes. Why did he always think of flowers when he was around her?

'I had an emergency. At home.' She spoke softly, warily.

'You lived on your own.' She didn't have kids. Not

that he knew of. Hell, he didn't even know if she had siblings.

'My mother was unwell.' She straightened her already straight spine and said, 'Andy was going places back then. Hard to believe he's now facing the fight of his life to remain alive, instead of continuing his work with paraplegics.'

What had been the problem with her mother? If he asked he doubted she'd tell him, and if she did then he'd know things about her that would make him feel connected with her. The last thing he wanted. Feeling responsible for her was not on his agenda. So, 'Andy's got a chance if he has the radical treatment they're offering him in California.'

'It must be hard for Kitty too.'

'Unimaginable.' Zac took a step closer to CC, ready to hug away that sadness glittering out at him. Sadness for their friend? Or her mother? Something had disturbed her cool facade.

Zac understood confronting situations that threatened to destroy a person. He'd been eighteen when the accident had happened that had left his brother, Mark, a paraplegic. Two years older than Mark, he was supposed to have been the sensible one. *Try being sensible with an out-of-control, aggressive younger brother intent on riling him beyond reason.* Nearly twenty years later the guilt could still swamp Zac, despite Mark having got on with his life, albeit a different one from what he'd intended before the accident.

The guilt was crippling. Being ostracised by his family because he'd been driving the car when it had slammed over the wall into the sea was as gutting. That's what put the shields over his heart. If his parents couldn't love him, who could? If he wasn't to be trusted to be responsible then he had no right to think any woman would be safe with him. Or any children he might have. So he had to keep from letting anyone near enough to undermine his determination to remain single, even when it went against all he believed in.

Olivia shuffled sideways, putting space between them. 'Here's hoping we raise a fortune tonight.'

Zac swallowed his disappointment, tried to find it in himself to be grateful Olivia had the sense to keep their relationship on an impersonal footing. It didn't come easily. He'd prefer to hug her, which wouldn't have helped either of them get past this tension that had gripped them from the instant he'd sauntered into the hotel. He wanted her, and suspected—no, he knew— she wanted him just as much. The one thing they'd been very good at had been reading each other's sexual needs. There hadn't been much else. Shallow maybe, but that's how they'd liked it. Their lives had been busy enough with work and study. Their careers had been taking off, leaving little time for much else.

But right now hugging Olivia would be wonderful. Why? He had no idea, but being this close to her he felt alive in a way he hadn't for months. Eighteen months, to be exact. This feeling wasn't about sex—though no denying he'd struggle to refuse if it was offered—but more about friendship and closeness. No, not close-ness. That would be dangerous. He hauled the armour back in place over his heart. One evening and the itch would be gone.

The elevator doors slid open quietly. Zac straight-ened from leaning against the wall, held his hand out to indicate to Olivia go first. 'After you.'

Following her, his gaze was firmly set on the backs of those wonderful legs and the sexy knee-length black boots highlighting them to perfection. Was it wrong to long for what they used to have? Probably not, but needing the closeness with her? That was different from anything he'd experienced, made him vulnerable. Earlier, seeing Olivia standing in Reception, looking like she had everything in hand, he'd felt the biggest lurch of his heart since the day his world had imploded as that car had sunk into the sea and his brother had screamed at him, 'I hate you.'

'Zac.' Olivia stopped, waited for him to come alongside her.

That slim neck he remembered so well was exposed where her coat fell open at her shoulders. 'CC.' If he used the nickname he might stop wanting something he couldn't have. This woman had already shown she could toss him aside as and when it suited her.

He watched as the tightness at the corners of her mouth softened into another heart-wrenching smile. 'Funny, I haven't been called CC for a while. I used to like having a nickname. More than anything else it made me feel I belonged to our group.'

'You never felt you belonged? Olivia, without you we wouldn't have had so many social excursions or parties. You held our year together.' She'd worked hard at organising fun times for them, sometimes taking hours away from her studies and having to make up for it with all-night sessions at her desk. But to feel she hadn't been an integral part of the group? How had he missed that?

Her smile turned wry. 'I've always taken charge. That way I'm not left out, and I get to call the shots. No one's going to ignore the leader, are they?'

His heart lurched again, this time for the little girl blinking out from those eyes staring at some spot behind him. He certainly didn't know this Olivia. 'I guess you're right.' With his family he'd learned what it felt like to be on the outside, looking in, but at university he'd made sure no one had seen that guy by working hard at friendships. A lot like Olivia apparently. Everyone at med school had adored her. She could be extroverted and fun, crazy at times, but never out of control. It was like she'd walked a tightrope between letting go completely and keeping a dampener on her feelings.

Except in bed—with him.

Damn, he'd like nothing more than to take Olivia to bed again. But it wouldn't happen. Too many consequences for both of them. The vulnerability in Olivia's eyes, her face, told him he could hurt her badly without even trying. That blew him apart. He wanted to protect her, not unravel her. *He cared about her.*

Trying to get away from Zac and her monumental error, Olivia rushed through the magnificent double doors opening into the banquet room now decorated in blue and white ribbons, table linen, chair covers. Since when did she go about telling people about her insecurities? Not even Zac—especially not Zac—had heard the faintest hint of how she didn't trust people not to trash her. She did things like this fundraiser so that people thought the best of her. That was the underlying reason she could not fail, would not have tonight be less than perfect. The same reason everything she did was done to her absolute best and then some. She must not be found lacking. Or stupid. Or needy.

Coming to a sudden halt, Olivia stared around the function room, which had been made enormous by sliding back a temporary wall. The sky-blue shade of Andy's favourite Auckland rugby team dominated. In the corner countless buckets of blue and white irises had finally been delivered and were waiting for the florist to arrange them in the clear glass bowls that were to go in the centre of each table. Everything was coming together as she'd planned it.

She was aware of Zac even before he said, 'Looking fantastic.'

Zac. Those few minutes in the elevator had been torture. Her nostrils had taken in his spicy aftershave, while her body had leaned towards his without any input from her brain. When he'd looked like he'd been about to hug her she'd at least had the good sense to move away, even when internally she'd been crying out to have those strong arms wound around her. Now she stamped a big smile on her face and acknowledged, 'It is.' Too bad if the smile didn't reach her eyes; hopefully Zac wouldn't notice.

'You're not happy about something.' He locked that formidable gaze onto her. 'Give.'

Once again she'd got it wrong when it came to second-guessing him. 'The florist's running late, the wineglasses haven't been set out, the band assured me they'd be set up by four and...' she glanced at her watch '...it's now three twenty-five.' *And you're distracting me badly. I want you. In my bed. Making out like we used to. Actually, I'd settle for that hug.*

'We can do this. Tell me what you want done first.' His eyes lightened with amusement, as if he'd read her mind.

He probably had. How well did she know him? Really? They hadn't been big on swapping notes on family or growing up or the things they were passionate about. Only the bedroom stuff. Shoving her phone at him, she said, 'Try the band. Their number's in there. Eziboys.'

'You've got the Eziboys coming to this shindig?'

Admiration gleamed out at her. 'What did you have to do? Bribe them with free plastic surgery for the rest of their lives?'

With a light punch to his bicep she allowed, 'One of them went to school with Andy's younger brother. They want to help the family.'

'Not your formidable charm, then?' He grinned a full-blown Zachary Wright grin, one that was famous for dropping women to their knees in a begging position.

Click, click. Her knees locked and she stayed upright. Just. 'Phone them, please.' Begging didn't count if she remained standing. Anyway, she wanted the band at the moment, not sex with this hunk in front of her looking like he'd stepped off the cover of a surfing magazine. Another lie.

Zac was already scrolling through her contact list. 'Got a dance card? I want the first one with you. And the second, third, and fourth. Oh, I know, I'll put those in your diary for tonight.'

Dance card, my butt. How out of date could he get? 'You'll be inundated with offers.' Did he really want to dance with her? She'd never survive. What little control she might exercise on her need would sink without trace if he so much as held her in his arms, let alone danced with her. Anyway, he wasn't making sense. He'd been peed off when she dumped him, so he wouldn't want to get close to her on the dance floor. Or did he have other plans? Plans that involved payback? Tease and tempt her, then say bye-bye?

As Zac put the phone to his ear he shook his head. 'If you didn't want dancing tonight you should've gone to the retirement village to find a group of old guys with their tin whistles to play for us.'

'I enjoy dancing.' *Just don't intend doing it with you.*

'I didn't know that. Looking forward to it. Looks like your florist has arrived.' He nodded in the direction of the doors, then went back to the phone. 'Jake, is that you, man? How're you doing?'

Olivia stared at Zac. He knew Jake Hamblin, the band's lead guitarist? That could be good for getting the band to actually turn up. Zac was full of surprises. Hadn't he said something about the florist too? Spinning around, she came face-to-face with a neat and tidy woman dressed in black tailored trousers and an angora jersey under her jacket. Nothing flower-like about her. 'You're the florist? I'm Olivia Coates-Clark.'

The woman nodded, sent Zac a grin. 'That's me. I see the flowers finally turned up. Show me exactly where you want these arrangements and I'll get on with it.'

Zac was handing the phone back to Olivia. 'How's things, Mrs Flower?' That really was her name. 'Your hip still working fine?'

'You were the surgeon. What do you think?'

Zac's laughter was loud and deep, and sent pangs of want kicking up a storm in Olivia's stomach. 'Good answer,' he said.

So he knew this woman too. Probably used her for sending beautiful flowers to all his women. Ouch. He'd sent her flowers when she'd dumped him. A stunning, colourful bouquet of peonies, not thorns or black roses, as well he might've.

'Do we have a band?' she asked in her best let's-get-on-with-things voice.

'Filling the service elevator with gear as we speak,' Zac said. 'What's next? Want those buckets of flowers moved somewhere?'

The band was on its way; the flowers were about

to be fixed. Olivia shook her head in amazement. Two more ticks on her mental list of outstanding things to get finished. Things just happened around Zac. Somehow it had all got easier with him here. 'We need two long tables up against that far wall for the auction. The hotel liaison officer went to find them an hour ago.' She needed to display the gifts that'd been donated.

'Not a problem.' Did he have to sound so relaxed?

The clock was ticking. That long soak she'd planned on in the big tub in her room upstairs before putting on her new dress, also from the shop where she'd got her coat, might just be a possibility. 'Easy for you to say,' she snapped.

Zac took her arm and led her across to where the florist was already wiring irises into clever bunches that were going to look exquisite. 'You explain where you want everything and try to relax. We'll get this baby up and running on time. That's a promise.'

'I am relaxed.'

'About as relaxed as a mouse facing down a cat. A big cat.' He grinned and strolled away before she could come up with a suitable rejoinder.

Very unlike her. She always had an answer to smart-ass comments. Watching Zac's casual saunter, she noted the way those wide shoulders filled his leather jacket to perfection. Her tongue moistened her lips. No wonder she wasn't thinking clearly—the distractions were huge and all came in one package. Zachary Wright.

CHAPTER THREE

AN HOUR LATER, Zac handed Olivia a champagne flute filled with bubbly heaven. 'Here, get that into you. It might help you unwind.'

'I can't drink now. I've got to finish in here, then get myself ready.' Her taste buds curled up in annoyance at being deprived of their favourite taste. But she had a big night ahead of her so having a drink before it had even begun was not a good idea.

With the proffered glass Zac nudged her hand—which seemed to have a life of its own as it reached towards him. 'One small drink will relax you, Olivia.' He wrapped her fingers around the cool stem. 'Go on.' There was a dare in his eyes as he raised his own glass to his lips.

Zac knew she never turned down a dare. But she'd have to. Tonight's success rested on her being one hundred and ten per cent on her game. Her mother had taught her well—go easy on the alcohol or make a fool of herself. Not going to happen tonight when everyone's eyes would be on her.

Zac's throat worked as he tasted the champagne. Appreciation lit up his eyes. His tongue licked his bottom lip.

And Olivia melted; deep inside where she'd stored all

her Zac memories there was a pool of hot, simmering need. The glass clinked against her teeth as the divine liquid spilled across her tongue. And while her shoulders lightened, tension of a different kind wound into a ball in her tummy and down to her core. 'Delicious,' she whispered. Zac or the wine?

He nodded. 'Yes, Olivia, it is. Now, take that glass upstairs to your room and have a soak in the hot tub before getting all glammed up. I'll see to anything else that needs to be done here before I go across to change.'

She went from relaxed to controlled in an instant. 'No. Thank you. I need to check on those flowers and—'

'All sorted.' From the table he handed her an iris that been tidied and then tied with a light blue ribbon. 'Take this up with you.'

Even as she hesitated, her hand was again accepting his gift. What was it with her limbs that they took no notice of her brain? 'My favourite flower.'

'That particular shade matches your eyes perfectly.'

'Wedgwood. That's the variety's name.' She stared at it, seeing things that had absolutely nothing to do with this weekend. Or Zac. All to do with her past.

When she made to hand it back he took her hand and held it between them, his fingers firm. His thumb caressed the inside of her wrist. 'Who does it remind you of?' Very perceptive of him.

How had she walked away from this man? She must've been incredibly strong that day, or very stupid. 'My father used to grow irises.' Before he'd left because he'd been unable to cope with his wife's drunken antics. *And I could? I was only twelve, Dad.*

Tugging free from Zac's hand, she stepped back a pace. 'Why are you helping me?' He hadn't decided to target her for sex, had he? Or was that her ego taking a hit? Zac never had trouble getting a woman; he didn't need her. Even if what they'd had between them had been off the planet.

Zac's eyes held something suspiciously like sympathy. She hated that. She didn't need it, had finally learned how to deal with her mother by controlling her own emotions, not her mother's antics. The same tactic kept men at a distance. Except for Zac, she'd managed very well. When she'd shocked herself one day by realising she cared about him more than she should she'd immediately called the whole thing off. No one would ever leave her again. No one could ever accuse her of being a slow learner.

'I'm here because you needed help.' Zac tapped the back of her hand to get her attention. 'I'm alone, as in no partner, so doing stuff behind the scenes isn't going to get anyone's back up. I figured you'd be pleased, not trying to get rid of me.'

I've already done that once.

The words hung in the air between them, as though she'd said them out loud. She hadn't, but her cheeks heated, as if she was blushing. Not something she was known for. 'I'm sorry for being an ungrateful cow.' She sipped from her glass while she gathered her scattered brain cells into one unit. 'It's great you're here. I'd still be trying to persuade that florist into doing things my way if you hadn't worked your magic on her.' She'd felt a tad ill at the ease with which he'd managed to convince the florist that her way was right. 'You also got that kid behind the bar to arrange the glasses in a much more spectacular pyramid than he'd intended.'

'While you charmed the floor manager into putting a dog basket in the corner for the seeing eye dog. It's against all the rules apparently.' Zac's smile was beautiful when he wasn't trying to win a favour. Too damned gorgeous for his own good. And hers.

'A blind person is allowed to take their dog anywhere.'

'But not necessarily have a bed for the night in the banquet room.' That smile just got bigger and better, and ripped through her like a storm unleashed.

She needed to get away before she did something as stupid as suggesting he give her a massage before she got dressed for the night. Zac's hands used to be dynamite when he worked on her muscles. He'd done a massage course sometime during his surgical training and was more than happy to share his ability with anyone needing a muscle or two unknotted. He'd done a lot more than that with her at times, but tonight she'd settle for a regular massage to get the strain and ache out of her shoulders.

Another lie. She gulped her drink, but forgot to savour the taste as the bubbles crossed her tongue. Lying wasn't something she normally did, not even to herself, as far as she knew.

'Here.' Zac held the champagne bottle in front of her, and leaned in to top up her glass. 'Take that up to your room.'

'You're repeating yourself.'

'Didn't think you'd got the message the first time.' Taking her elbow, he began marching her towards the elevators where he pressed the up button, and when the doors whooshed open he nudged her in. 'See you at pre-dinner drinkies.'

'I'll be down well before six.' As the doors closed quietly Oliva drew in his scent and along with it a whole heap more memories. The night ahead was stretching out ever further. She'd tried again to change the seat-ing arrangement at the tables, but couldn't without upsetting someone else. She sighed. Have to swallow that one and hope she'd be too busy to sit down.

Olivia tapped the toe of her boot until the elevator eased to a halt on her floor. Surprisingly she had nearly an hour to herself, thanks to Zac's help. Plenty of time to wrestle into submission the strong emotions she'd never expected to feel for him again. Then she could carry on as planned: friendly yet aloof. So far her approach had been a big fail.

Inside her room she began shedding clothes as she headed for the bathroom and the tub she wanted full, steaming and bubbling.

After turning the taps on full, she poured in a hefty dose of bubble bath and shucked out of the rest of her clothes. Removing her make-up, she saw a goofy smile and happier eyes in the mirror than she'd seen in a very long time.

Hey, be careful.

Why was she excited? She didn't want another affair with the man. It had been hard enough walking away from the first one; to do that again would kill her. Even though their affair had had little to do with anything other than sex, she'd stumbled through the following weeks trying to get back on track. It had her wondering for the millionth time how her father had walked out on her and her mother without a backward glance. He'd had more to lose, yet every communication from him—not many—had come through a lawyer. No birthday cards, Christmas phone calls. Nothing. Her dad had vanished from her life. And that was that.

Slipping into the warm water and feeling the bubbles tickle her chin eased every last knot of tension from her taut body. Sure, it'd make a comeback, but for the next twenty minutes she'd enjoy the lightness now in her muscles, her tummy, her everywhere. That might help with facing Zac tonight.

Olivia knew she had to be on her best form because their friends wouldn't be able to refrain from watching her and Zac, looking for any hints of dissension or, worse, any sign they might be interested in each other again. Not a chance, folks.

Lying back, her eyes drifted shut and she watched the movie crossing her mind. Zac looking good enough to devour in one sitting. That well-honed body still moved like a panther's, wary yet smooth, the same as the expression in his eyes. Unbelievable how much she'd missed that body. Missed everything about Zac. There'd been the odd occasion they'd shared a meal, because when anyone had had as much exercise as they'd had together they'd got hungry and what had gone best with after-match lethargy had been great food. Ordered in from some of Auckland's best restaurants, of course. The only way to go.

What she'd never seen in his eyes before was that concern that had shown when he'd moved her towards the elevator. Concern for her well-being, and then there had been the flower, the champagne—which had shown he'd remembered she only drank wine, and then usually this nectar. Yes, she pampered herself, but there was no one else to. Except her mother, and she got her fair share of being looked after.

Was it possible Zac had missed her an incy-wincy bit? She'd never ask. That would be like setting a match to petrol. Anyway, he'd never admit it, even if it came close to being true.

Hah, like you'd admit it either.

* * *

Zac prowled the small crowd pouring into the banquet room, and for the tenth time glanced at his watch. Six o'clock had been and gone twenty minutes ago and there was no sign of Olivia. So unlike her. If anything, she'd have been back down here, ready to get things cranking up, almost an hour before it was supposed to start.

'Hey, Zac, good to see you.' Paul Entwhistle stepped in front of him. 'How have you been?'

'Paul.' Zac shook his old mentor's hand. 'I'm doing fine. What about you? Still creating merry hell down there at Waikato?' The older man had taken over as director of the orthopaedic unit two years ago, citing family reasons for leaving the successful private practice he'd set up here in Auckland.

Paul gave him an easy smile. 'I've semiretired to spend more time with the family. What about you? I couldn't believe it when I heard you and Olivia had parted. Thought you'd never be able to untangle yourselves long enough to go in different directions.'

Zac swallowed a flare of annoyance. This was only the first of what he had no doubt would be many digs tonight about his past with Olivia. 'Aren't we full of surprises, then?' Instantly he wished his words back. Paul had been a friend to him as well as teaching him complex surgical procedures that he now used regularly. The man certainly didn't deserve his temper. He tried again. 'There was so much going on at the time something had to give.'

That was one way of looking at it. He knew from friends that Olivia ran with the crowd these days and never with another man. He didn't get it. She'd been fun, and always hungry for a good time. But apparently not since *them*. Did that make him responsible for her change? Had he done something he was completely unaware of to cause her to dump him and become a solo act? He'd always been honest in that he'd had no intention of having anything more than a fling with her. She'd been of the same sentiment. Neither of them had been interested in commitment. Yet it still sucked big time that she'd pulled out. He hadn't thought he could feel so vulnerable. Why would he? He'd spent his life guarding against that.

'I get that, but never thought it would be your relationship that would stop.' Paul unwittingly repeated Zac's thoughts as he looked around the room. 'Where is Olivia anyway?'

Twenty-five past six. 'I have no idea. I'll give her a call.' Walking away to find somewhere quieter, he dialled her cell. Yes, he still had her numbers, just never used them. Deleting them should've been simple, but he hadn't been able to, even when he'd been angry with her for walking away.

'Hey, Zac, I fell asleep.' So she still had him on caller ID. Interesting. 'Is everything okay? I'll be right down.' Olivia sounded breathless.

He knew the breathless version, had heard it often as they'd made love. 'Breathe deep and count to ten. Everything's going according to your plan.'

'Yes, but I need to be there, welcoming everyone. Oh, damn.' He heard a clatter in the background. 'Damn, damn, triple damn.'

'Olivia, are you all right?'

'I knocked my glass off the side of the tub. Now there are shards of glass all over the floor.'

'Call Housekeeping.'

'Haven't got time. I'm meant to be down there before everyone arrives, not after, as though I don't care.' Panic mixed with anger reached his ear. 'How could I be so stupid as to fall asleep in the tub?'

'Listen to me.' Zac stared up at the high ceiling, trying hard not to visualise *that* picture. Olivia in a hot tub with soapy bubbles framing her pert chin, covering her full breasts. *Aw, shucks.*

'I worked every hour there was to get this gala happening and I'm tired, but I only had to hang on for a few more hours.' She was on a roll, and Zac knew it would take a bomb to shut her up.

He delivered. 'I'm coming up to help you get ready.' Like Olivia would let him in. She hated being out of control over any damned thing and would be wound up tighter than a gnat's backside.

'You can't come up here,' she spluttered. 'I'm not dressed.'

So his words *had* hit the bull's-eye. She'd heard him. He found himself smiling, and not just externally. Warmth was expanding, turning him all gooey. Bonkers. This was all wrong.

Zac told her, 'Take your time getting ready, then make a grand entrance. Everyone will be here and you can wow them as you walk to the podium to make the opening announcements.'

There was utter silence at the other end of the phone. No more spluttering. No glasses smashing on the tiled floor. Not even Olivia breathing. Then his smile spread into a grin. He could almost hear her mind working.

'Love it,' she said, and hung up on him.

Zac slid his phone back in the pocket of his evening suit trousers. He guessed he'd see her shortly. Heading back into the room, he hesitated as the elevator doors opened. Seeing the pale, thin man who stepped out, he crossed over to shake his hand. 'Hey, Andy, great to see you.' The guy looked dreadful. Leukaemia was making short work of his health.

'Isn't this something? I couldn't believe it when Olivia told me how many people were coming and all the amazing things that have been donated for the auction.' Andy wiped a hand down his face. 'Enough to make a bloke cry.'

'Can't have that, man.' Zac dredged up a grin for him, feeling a lump rising in his own throat. 'You'll have all the females copying you.'

Andy laughed, surprising Zac. 'Damn right there. What sort of dinner party would that be? They'd be handing round tissues, not champagne.'

'Guess you're off the drink at the moment.' Zac glanced behind, and saw Kitty and their three small boys waiting calmly. 'Great to see you.' He wrapped the woman in his arms and when he felt her shivering he knew it was from trepidation about tonight. 'You're doing fine,' he said quietly, so only she heard.

Kitty nodded. 'Thanks to CC. She's arranged a table for us and the boys, a babysitter for when it's time to send the little tykes to our suite, and basically anything we could possibly want.'

'That's our CC.' *Damn you, Olivia. A man could fall in love with you—if he hadn't locked his heart in a cage. You've done the most amazing and generous thing, arranging this evening.* 'Come on, I'll show you to your table.' Andy looked ready to collapse and they hadn't started.

It took time to move through the throng of people wishing the family all the best for the auction. Zac knew everyone meant well and most were shocked at Andy's appearance, but he wanted to snarl at them to back off and give the man time to settle at his table. He held onto his sudden burst of temper, wondering where it had come from in the first place.

As he finally pulled out a chair for Kitty a collective gasp went up around the large room. Olivia had arrived. He hadn't seen her but he knew. She had that effect on people, on him. Like lightning she zapped the atmosphere, flashed that dazzling smile left, right and centre. Everyone felt her pull; fell under her spell. Which was why they were here, and why many had willingly donated such spectacular gifts for the auction. She was the reason these same people would soon be putting their hands in their pockets and paying the earth for those things. Sure, this was all about Andy, a man everyone liked and respected, but it was Olivia who'd got them all together.

Looking towards the podium, Zac thought he'd died and gone to heaven. Never, ever, in those crazy weeks he and Olivia had been getting down and dirty had he seen her look like she did right this moment. If he had he'd have hauled her back to his bedroom that last night and tied her to the bed so she couldn't dump him. He'd have taken a punt on her not breaking his heart even when it was obvious she would've. Stunning didn't begin to describe her. And that dress? Had to be illegal. Didn't it? She shouldn't be allowed to wear it in public. It appeared painted on, except for where the soft, weightless fabric floated across her thighs. Everywhere her body was highlighted with the gold material shimmering over her luscious curves.

And he'd thought he could handle this evening, being around Olivia. He hadn't a hope in Hades. Not one.

CHAPTER FOUR

'WELCOME, EVERYONE, TO what is going to be a wonderful night.' Olivia stood behind the podium, the mic in her hand, and let some of the tension slide across her lips on a low breath. She'd done it. Andy and his family were here, the colleagues who'd said they'd come were here, and the noise level already spoke of people having fun. Phew.

Zac's here. So? She knew that already.

Olivia could see him standing by Andy, staring over at her, his mouth hanging a little loosely. He looked stunned. What had put that expression on his face? Not her, surely? She stepped out from behind the podium, shifted her hips so that her dress shimmied over her thighs, and watched Zac. Forget stunned. Try knocked out. She bet a whole team of cheerleaders could be leaping up and down naked in front of him right now and he wouldn't notice. His gaze was intense and totally fixed on her. Or, rather, on her thighs.

Despite being like nothing else she'd worn since she'd been a teen, she'd loved this dress from the moment she'd seen it; now she thought it was the best outfit ever created. That sex thing she and Zac had once had going? It was still there, alive and well, already fired up and ready to burn.

Then the silence reached her and she stared around at the gathering of friends and colleagues, the reason she was standing up here finally returning to her bemused brain. She was supposed to be wowing them, not getting slam-dunked by Zac's comatose expression. Slapping her forehead in front of everyone wasn't a good idea, but she did it anyway. 'Sorry, everyone, I forgot where I was for a moment. Thought I was back at med school and about to give you all a demo on how to drink beer while standing on my head.' Like she'd ever done anything close.

But it got her a laugh and she could relax. As long as she didn't look in Zac's direction she should be able to continue with her brief outline of how the evening would unfold.

'I hope you've all got your bank managers' phone numbers handy because we are going to have the auction of all auctions. It will be loads of fun, but just to get you loosened up there are limitless numbers of champagne flutes filled with the best drop of nectar doing the rounds of the room. Stop any of those handsome young men carrying trays and help yourself.'

She paused, and immediately her eyes sought Zac. He hadn't moved, still stood watching her, but at least he'd stopped looking like a possum caught in headlights. His eyes were hooded now, hiding whatever had been eating him, and that delicious mouth had tightened a little. Then he winked, slowly with a nod at the room in general.

She got the message. *Get on with it. Everyone's waiting for you.*

Again she looked around the room filled with people she knew, admired and in a lot of cases really liked. 'Just to keep us all well behaved and lasting the distance, there will be platters of canapés arriving over the next hour. We will have the auction before dinner so take a look at all the wonderful gifts set out on the tables over by the entrance. Most importantly, enjoy yourselves, but not until I've kept hotel management happy by telling you what to do in case of fire, earthquake, or the need to use a bathroom.'

After giving those details, she wrapped up. 'Let's have a darned good time. If there's anything that you feel you're missing out on talk to...' she looked around the room and of course her gaze fell on Zac '...Zachary Wright. He's volunteered to help with any problems and we'd hate to see him sitting around with nothing to do, wouldn't we?' She grinned over at the man who'd got her stomach in a riot. Not only her stomach, she conceded, while trying to ignore the smug smile coming back at her. Not easy to do when her heart rate was erratic. The noise levels were rising fast as she stepped away from the podium to go in search of a distraction that didn't begin with a Z.

Paul Entwhistle stepped in front of her. 'Olivia, you're a marvel, girl. There's as many people here as you'd find at Eden Park watching an international rugby match.' He wrapped her into a bear hug. 'Well done.'

'Still prone to exaggerating, I see.' She laughed as she extricated herself. 'Are you going to be bidding at the auction? There are some wonderful prizes—if I can call them that.'

'I've got my eye on one or two.' There was a cunning glint in Paul's eyes.

'What?'

Paul went with a complete change of subject. 'I see you still like to give Zac a bit of stick. It saddened me when you two broke up. Thought you had what it took.'

Her stomach sucked in against her backbone. *Not in this lifetime, we don't.* But even as she thought it her eyes were tracking the crowd for a dark head. Not hard to find when Zac towered above most people, even the tall ones. He was heading in her direction, an amused tilt to his mouth. 'I beg to differ,' she told Paul. 'Neither of us are the settling-down type.' *If only that weren't true.* 'Now, if you'll excuse me...'

'I think you're wrong.' Paul glanced in the direction she'd seen Zac. The cunning expression had changed to something more whimsical, which didn't make her feel any more comfortable.

'I need to circulate.' *Before Zac reaches us.* 'I'm sure Zac will be happy to chat with you.'

'Thanks a bundle, Olivia,' Zac breathed into her ear. Too late. She plastered on a smile and faced him, wondering why just talking to him got her all in a twist. 'Thought you'd be pleased. You're flying solo, remember?'

He actually laughed. 'Touché.'

Paul was watching them with interest. She really needed to stop this; whatever the man was thinking didn't have a part in the evening's plans.

'I have to see the auctioneer about a few details,' Olivia put out there, and began walking away.

'Are we going to be holding up the various items as they're auctioned?' Zac was right beside her.

She was regretting giving in to his offer of help—if she had actually given in. He hadn't exactly left it open to negotiation. 'I'm doing it.'

'Then we're doing it.' His hand on her arm brought her to a stop. When he turned her to face him his eyes were full of genuine concern. For her? Or did he think she was going to make a mess of the evening? 'I know you've done everything so far and by rights this is your show, but I'd like to help. And I'm not the only one. Andy's been a good mate to a lot of people.'

'That's a valid point.' Didn't mean she'd hand over the reins, though. When she set out to do something she did the whole thing, from first phone call to seeing the last couple leave at the end of the night. That would give her a deep sense of accomplishment, something she never achieved with trying to keep her mother on the straight and narrow.

Zac's bowed upper lip curved into a heart-squeezing smile. 'Let's grab a drink and go talk to your auctioneer.'

For some reason Zac made her feel desirable on a different level from the hot need she usually found in his gaze. That was there, burning low and deep, but right now she could have curled up on a couch with him and just chatted about things. Not something they'd ever done before. Had never wanted to do. Shaking her head, she gave him a return smile. 'I'll stick to water until I've packed up this baby.'

Without looking away from her, he raised his hand and suddenly there was a waiter with a tray of full glasses standing beside them. Zac lifted two flutes of sparkling water and handed her one. Tapping his glass against hers, he gave her another of those to-die-for smiles. 'To making a load of money for our friend.'

'Lots and lots.' She sipped the water, and tried not to sneeze when bubbles somehow went up her nose. The bubbles won, and she bent her head to brazen out the sneezes.

Her glass was gently removed from her hand as Zac's firm, warm hand touched her between her shoulder blades, warm skin on warm skin, softly rubbing until she regained control. Straightening up, she reached for her glass and locked eyes with Zac. 'Th-thanks,' she stuttered.

How could she speak clearly with so much laughter and fun beaming out at her from a pair of eyes the shade of her first coffee of the day? Those eyes had always got her attention, had had her melting with one glance. For some strange reason tonight they had her fantasising about other, homier things. Like that couch and talking, or sharing a meal over the table in her kitchen, or going for a stroll along the beach. *A bit cosy, Olivia. What happened to forgoing doing things like that with someone special?* 'You ever think of settling down?' she asked, before she'd thought the question through.

His expression instantly became guarded. 'Thought about it? Yes. Followed through? No.'

Oh. Disappointment flared, which didn't make sense when she never intended putting her size five shoes under someone's bed. Not permanently anyway. 'That's sad.' For Zac. He'd make a wonderful husband and father.

'Not at all. I'm happy.' So why the sadness lurking in the back of those dark eyes?

'You sound very sure.' Her blood slowed as her heart slipped up on its pumping habit. Strange that here, surrounded by friends and colleagues, Zac was admitting to not wanting happy-ever-after.

'I am,' he muttered, as he took her elbow and led them in the direction of the auction table and the man standing behind it. 'Just as I'm sure I'm enjoying playing catch-up with you.'

Okay. Hadn't seen that coming. 'We could've done that any time.' What? Since when? She'd been ruthless in avoiding Zac, turning down invitations to any functions she'd thought he might be attending. The air in her lungs trickled out over her bottom lip. Now he stood beside her she couldn't keep her eyes off him. He warmed her through and through, touching her deeply, like a close friend. Except friends didn't do what they'd done, and sex-crazed lovers like they'd been didn't sit around discussing fashion or trips to the supermarket. But she told him anyway. 'I've sort of settled, bought a nineteen-twenties villa in Parnell that I'm slowly doing up.' *My own house, all mine.*

Zac's eyes widened. 'Are you working the do-up yourself?'

'I've got a very good builder for most of it, while I do the painting and wallpapering. Seems I've got a bit of a flair for home decorating.' She felt a glow of pride when she thought of her new kitchen and dining alcove.

'Go, you.'

'Hi, Olivia.' The auctioneer, Gary, held out his hand. 'You've got an amazing array of donations. We should be able to pull off a major coup.'

'That's the plan.' Shaking Gary's hand, she introduced Zac. 'Anything we can do for you?'

'You can take a break and leave this to me and my partner over there. He's come along to help.' Gary nodded at a man sorting through the donations and placing numbers under each one. 'Just keep our glasses full and we'll be happy.'

Zac's hand was back on her elbow. 'Come on, let's mingle.'

She could do that on her own. Yet she went with him as if that was the most important thing she had to do tonight.

Zac groaned inwardly. He should be running for the exit and not looking back. Standing beside Olivia as she charmed everyone within sight was sending him bonkers with need. Every time she moved even a single muscle he'd swear he inhaled her scent. She moved almost nonstop, even when standing in one spot, her face alive, with those lips constantly forming belly-tightening smiles while her eyes sparkled. Her free hand flipped up and down, then out between her and her audience, and back in against her gorgeous body, expressive at every turn.

While one of his hands was shoved deep into his pocket to keep from touching her, the other gripped a glass tight. His feet were glued to the carpet, and his face hopefully impassive. Letting anyone, especially CC, know what he was thinking and feeling would be catastrophic. He'd never hear the end of it from Paul either. The guy stood with them, his gaze flitting between him and Olivia with a crafty glint that made Zac uncomfortable.

A waiter was approaching with a tray laden with glasses. Zac drained his sparkling water and replaced it with champagne. To hell with not drinking. He needed something stronger than H2O, bubbles or not. 'Thanks.' He nodded at the waiter, which was a waste of time.

The guy was too busy gaping at Olivia, the tray on his outstretched fingers getting quite a tilt. 'Ma'am,' the young man croaked.

Totally understanding the poor guy's reaction, Zac tapped the tray. 'Hey, buddy, watch those glasses.'

Olivia swapped her empty glass for a full one, nodded at the waiter, and looked around the room as she gulped a mouthful of water.

Zac saw some of the tension in her neck ease off a notch. Being a perfectionist, CC didn't do relaxing very well, and tonight she was coiled tighter than a snake about to strike.

'Time to start the auction,' Olivia said in a sudden gap of the conversation. 'I think everyone must be here by now.'

'Good idea,' Paul said. 'Make the most of this amazing atmosphere.' He nodded at the crowd talking and laughing.

'Why don't we hold up the articles being auctioned while Gary's man deals with the financial side?' Zac led the way through the throng to the podium.

Olivia nodded, picked up the mic. 'Okay, everyone, can I have your attention?'

Nope. Not happening. If anything, the noise level seemed to increase. Zac reached for the mic, touching the back of her hand as he did so. Soft, warm, different Olivia. His mouth dried. It wasn't too late. He could still run away. And then what? Spend the night thinking about Olivia and coming up with a hundred questions about her?

Clearing his throat, he spoke loudly and clearly into the mic. 'Quiet, please.' The conversations petered out as everyone turned to face him. He wanted to crack a joke but doubted he could pull it off with this tight band strangling his throat. If only Olivia would move away and let him breathe. Finally he started talking and slowly got his voice back to normal. 'We are about to start the auction so take a seat. Gary is our auctioneer and we want him to be able see each and every one of you, so even if you scratch your knee he can take it as a bid.'

As the bidding got under way Olivia's tension climbed back up. 'Relax,' he told her. 'This is going to be amazing, you'll see.'

She turned worried eyes on him. 'How can you be so certain? What if we barely raise enough money to get Andy a one-way ticket to the States?' Her teeth nibbled her bottom lip.

Olivia didn't do nibbling. Taking her hand in his, he squeezed gently. 'I believe in you, that's how.'

Her eyes widened, her chin tipped forward. 'Truly?' she squeaked.

'Truly.' He did. He realised that through the years they'd been training to become surgeons he mightn't have noticed how sexy she was but he had known of her determination never to fail. Perhaps he hadn't learned much more about her during their affair but this was still Olivia, the same woman who'd qualified as an excellent plastic surgeon. Only now he saw how much she cared for their friends. Olivia was a big marshmallow, really, and he liked marshmallows.

'Thanks.'

'Olivia? So do all the people in this room. That's why they're here.'

He felt a responding squeeze where her hand was wound around his. 'You say the nicest things,' she whispered, before pulling free and turning to face the now-quiet room.

She'd been flip in her tone and yet it didn't bother him. That was Olivia covering her real feelings. He was beginning to see she was an expert at doing that. Come to think about it, she'd always shut him up with a kiss whenever he'd started to talk about anything personal. What was she hiding? Who was Olivia Coates-Clark? The real CC?

As Zac picked up the envelope to be auctioned, which contained a week in a timeshare bure in Fiji, he knew he was getting into trouble. Forget quietening the itch. Now he had to fight the need to get to know all about Olivia, right from when she'd lost her first tooth to what her idea was of a dream holiday.

The bidding was fast and furious, with plenty of people vying to buy the first offering. In the end Paul outbid everyone, paying enough to send a dozen folks to Fiji rather than the two that the deal covered.

'That's auctions for you,' Zac whispered to Olivia as at last she began smiling.

'It's not about what they're bidding for, is it?'

'Nope. It's all about the man sitting at that table with his wife and kids, looking like hell and pretending otherwise.' Andy looked shocked, actually. Probably because of the ridiculous amount Paul had bid.

Olivia nudged him. 'We're not a bad bunch, are we?'

'Apart from opinionated, hardworking, and overly comfortable with our lot, you mean?' He grinned at her.

'I'd like to think more along the lines of caring, hardworking, and overly focused on helping others.' She grinned back.

His stomach clenched. That grin, that mouth…oh, man. *I've missed her so much.* Not just the sex. He'd liked being with her too, even if only while they'd ridden the elevator to the apartment she'd rented then, and before they'd fallen into bed.

'What are we auctioning next?' he growled, needing to get back on an even keel.

'The weekend on your luxury yacht. If you're at the helm that should attract a lot of female bidders.' Her grin only grew.

'The ladies here are all taken.' *Except you.* Zac sighed when one of the partners in the surgical practice where he worked bought the weekend excursion.

The man wasn't easy to get along with, and now he'd have to spend two days holed up in a yacht with him and his whole family.

'You're being uncharitable,' Olivia whispered beside his ear.

'I didn't say a word.'

'There was a brief wincing and tightening of your mouth when the hammer hit the podium.' She laughed. 'That man paid a small fortune for the pleasure of going sailing with you.'

'He did, and I'll make sure he has a fantastic time.'

Gary had the crowd in the palm of his hand now, and the bidding went through the roof for everything from a painting of a seagull hovering over a beach to a meal at a restaurant down at the Viaduct Harbour.

Zac watched Olivia every time the gavel hit the podium. Her eyes were getting brighter and brighter. 'We're killing it,' she whispered at one point.

'Says the woman who was worried this wouldn't work,' he retorted. The more she smiled the more she relaxed, and the more beautiful she was. Zac felt his heart soften even further towards her. So he sucked in his stomach and hardened himself against her. Mentally, that was.

'That's me. Control freak with no control over the outcome of the auction. Of course I was going to be concerned.'

Was that why she'd ended their affair? So she could keep control and not wait until he decided to call it quits? Since the morning he'd woken to hear Olivia say she was walking away from their affair he'd felt bruised and let down. He hadn't known why, except it had reminded him of the day his family had cut him off. But with Olivia he'd had nothing to feel guilty about.

'That's it, folks. We've sold everything,' Gary called out.

Olivia crossed to stand behind the podium, a piece of paper in her hand, tears in her eyes. 'You're an amazing group of people. This auction went way beyond even my dreams.' She read out the amount they'd raised and had to wait a long time for the applause to die down. 'You are all so generous it's humbling.'

Zac glanced across to Andy's table, and felt emotion tug at his heart. Kitty was crying and Andy slashed his arm across his face as he slowly stood up. Carefully negotiating his way around tables to reach Olivia, Andy gave her a long hug before gripping Zac's shoulder.

'Hey.' Zac could think of nothing else to say. The success of the auction said everything that needed to be said about the love he felt for this man.

Taking the mic, Andy stumbled to the podium. 'What can I say? Olivia's right. You're awesome.' His voice cracked. 'Tonight means so much to Kitty and me, and our boys. You have given us a chance.' He stopped and looked down. Everyone waited quietly until he raised his head and said, 'CC, I can't thank you enough. I know so many people contributed to tonight and I thank each and every one of them, but without you, CC, none of this would've happened.'

Zac clapped and instantly everyone leapt to their feet to join him. He reached for Olivia's hand and raised it high. 'Our CC.'

Tears were streaming down her cheeks. 'Stop it,' she hissed. 'You're embarrassing me.'

Zac retrieved the mic from Andy and when the clapping died down said, 'In case you missed that, CC says we're embarrassing her. When did that ever happen?'

Laughter and more clapping broke out. Olivia shook her head at him. 'You'll keep.'

There was the problem. He shouldn't want to be kept for Olivia. Or any woman. He wouldn't be able to deliver what she wanted, needed.

CHAPTER FIVE

'DID YOU JUST YAWN?' Zac asked as they danced to the Eziboys' music.

Olivia shook her head. 'Just doing mouth stretches.' Did there have to be a smile in his eyes? It was devastating in its intensity. Made her happy to be with him, when she shouldn't be. Exhaustion had returned as dessert had come to an end, yet somehow she'd still found the energy to shake her hips to the beat of the music.

Zac's eyes widened, and the tip of his tongue appeared at the corner of his delectable mouth. 'Right,' he drawled.

She mentally slapped her head. Mouth stretches. She used to trail kisses all over his body, starting below his ear and tracking down, down, down. The memories were vivid now, in full technicolour, and heating up her cheeks. Hopefully he wouldn't notice her heightened colour in the semidarkness of the dance floor.

It would take very little to fall in against that wide chest and let him be her strength for a while. She'd never known what it was like to let someone be strong for her. If she ever loosened up enough to try it, Zac might be her man.

How had she managed to leave him that morning? Fear. Always a powerful motivator. For her it had been fear of losing control, of never knowing which way was up. As an adult she had no intention of reliving the turbulent life she'd known growing up. Not for anyone.

'Feel like taking a break, having a drink?' Zac asked.

Definitely. Anything to put some space between them. 'Good idea.' She immediately turned for their table.

Waving at a waiter, Zac pulled out a chair. 'Take the weight off.'

When he sat down beside her his chair was way too close, but she was reluctant to make a show of moving away. Anyway, she didn't have the strength to resist him at the moment. Glancing at her watch, she sighed. The band was booked for at least another hour. Sneaking off to her room and that huge comfortable-looking bed was not yet an option.

The champagne was cool and delicious. 'Perfect.' She settled further into her chair. 'You keep dancing, if you want. I don't need babysitting.'

Zac chuckled. 'Dancing has never been one of my favourite pastimes.'

'But you're good at it. You've got the moves.' *Ouch.* Shouldn't have said that.

That devastating smile returned briefly. 'I'd say thanks except you seemed to nearly fall asleep while we were shaking our hips.'

'I can't believe how tired I am. Probably won't go to sleep for hours when I finally make it to my room. My muscles feel like they're pulled tighter than a tourniquet.'

'What you need is a few days away somewhere where no one can reach you to talk about work, or fundraising, or anything more stressful than what you'd like for dinner.' Zac sipped his drink. 'When did you last take time off?'

She thought about it. Glanced at him. Remembered. 'It was a while ago.'

'A little over eighteen months ago maybe?'

'Maybe.' Zac had booked three nights at a retreat on Waiheke Island. They'd only managed one night before he'd returned home after his brother had been admitted to hospital with a collapsed lung.

While accepting he had to go, Olivia had been disappointed he'd not returned to the resort later. She sometimes wondered—if they'd had the whole time together would they have got to know each other a little better outside the bedroom?

'I might as well have stayed with you,' Zac muttered, as if reading her mind.

Olivia's stomach flipped. 'What? Your family needed you.' So had she, but not as much.

'No, they didn't.'

'But they phoned you.'

He shook his head. 'My grandfather called to let me know about Mark. Not my parents.'

She wanted to say that made sense if his parents had rushed to be with his brother, but something in his eyes stopped her, told her she was wrong. 'You don't get along—'

'Mind if I join you both for a moment?' Paul plonked himself down without waiting for an answer.

Relief flicked across Zac's face. 'Can I get you a drink, Paul?'

'No, thanks. I won't take up much of your time.' Leaning back in the chair, he studied first Zac then her so thoroughly she began to think she had chocolate mousse on her chin.

The band stopped for a short break and most people were making their way to the tables. And Paul still wasn't saying anything. She ran her fingers across her chin, came up clean. She glanced at Zac, who shrugged his shoulders.

Finally, Paul pulled an envelope from the inside pocket of his jacket and Olivia instantly recognised it as an item that had been auctioned earlier. A trip somewhere. There'd been a few trips auctioned tonight but she thought Paul's one had been to Fiji.

As he laid the envelope on the table between her and Zac she felt a flutter of trepidation in her stomach. She couldn't keep her eyes off that large white envelope or the finger tapping it, as though it was beating out her fate.

'This is for the two of you. Five nights at Tokoriki Island Resort on the west side of Fiji's mainland.'

No. No, please, no. Tell me Paul didn't say that. I can't go anywhere with Zac, and certainly not somewhere as intimate as a resort in Fiji.

Olivia slowly raised her gaze to Zac and saw him looking as stunned as she felt. 'It's kind of you, Paul, but I have to say no.'

'Zac? What do you think?' Paul looked a little smug.

It didn't matter what Zac thought. She wasn't going.

A few days far away from everything and everyone with only Zac for company held a certain appeal. White beaches, warm sea, palm trees bending in the breeze, and... And Zac.

'It's a no from me too. Thank you, though.'

Paul wasn't easily fobbed off. 'Think before rejecting my offer out of hand, both of you.'

Olivia shook her head. One evening with Zac had her

in a state of longing and wonder. She would never cope with being stuck on a tiny island with him for a week.

'What's this about?' Zac asked in a surprisingly level tone, his eyes fixed on the man issuing the challenge.

'Look at you. You're exhausted. I know you haven't had a break all year. You need a holiday. So does Olivia. Why not someplace exotic? This timeshare bure is on an island catering for approximately twenty couples at any one time. No children allowed. All meals provided, massages as well.' Paul smiled.

Any other time she'd be drooling at the thought of going. But never with the man sitting beside her, looking as perplexed as she felt.

'It sounds wonderful, but you're expecting Zac and me to go together?' Olivia shook her head. *Not going to happen.* Looking at Zac, she could see the lines at the edges of his mouth. He *was* tired. It had taken Paul pointing it out for her to notice.

'You have two weeks to choose between, both in July, so you'll need to get your heads together quickly.'

Which part of 'I'm not going' doesn't Paul understand? 'July's two weeks away. I can't just pack my bag and leave my patients in the lurch.'

'Neither can I,' Zac growled.

Paul hadn't finished. 'I'll cover for you, Zac, and I'm sure we can find someone to pick up the reins in your department for five days, CC.'

'You still haven't said why you're doing this. Us needing a holiday doesn't cover such generosity.' Zac sipped his drink, a thoughtful expression on his handsome face.

An expression that worried Olivia. He'd better not be considering this crazy idea. She snapped, 'It doesn't matter why. It's not going to happen.' Knowing how ungrateful that sounded, and yet annoyed that Paul thought he could manipulate them, she added, 'It's a lovely offer, Paul, but I'm turning you down.'

The moment the words left her mouth she was regretting the lost opportunity. A holiday would be fabulous right now. Keeping up her usual number of patients and working on this gala fundraiser had finally caught up with her. Throw in her mum's latest crisis, and heading offshore to somewhere she'd be pampered sounded better and better. A sideways glance at Zac and she couldn't deny that going away with him didn't have appeal. Her head snapped up. *She was not going anywhere with Zac.*

Someone coughed. 'I'll cover for you, Olivia.' A colleague at Auckland Surgical Hospital sat on the other side of the table, looking completely relaxed about the whole scenario. 'You know you've been wanting to get away for a while now. The timing couldn't be better. Leave it another couple of months and I'll be on maternity leave.'

Thanks a million. You obviously haven't heard the whole conversation, especially the bit about Zac going too. But as Olivia glared at the woman she felt herself wavering. This might be working out too easily, but did that mean she shouldn't be considering it? Should she be grabbing that envelope and rushing home to pack, or was it wiser to continue refusing Paul's kindness?

Zac was watching her with something akin to an annoying challenge in his eyes. 'What about it, CC? It could be fun.'

'It could be a nightmare.' How would she remain aloof when they were sharing accommodation on an island with very few people around for distraction? How would she be able to control herself with that hot bod so close for days on end?

Pulling her gaze from that infuriating taunt in Zac's eyes, she looked around the now-crowded table and found everyone watching, waiting for her answer, almost as though they were all challenging her.

You never turn down a dare, remember?

She'd never had one quite like this, though. She could not go on holiday with the man she'd had to walk away from once already. Not when he'd got her in a tangle of emotions within minutes of turning up in the hotel earlier that afternoon. She'd never survive with her heart and her brain functioning normally if she spent five days and nights in the same space as Zac.

You'd have a lot of great sex.

Not necessarily. They could avoid that. It wasn't as though they were going *together*-together, right?

Tell that to someone who'll believe you.

The little gremlin that had flattened her car battery and made her fall asleep in the hot tub now had her saying, 'It would have to be the first week of July.'

Zac shoved his hands deep into his trouser pockets as he strolled along the Viaduct beside Olivia. At one-thirty in the morning, in the middle of winter, they were the only ones crazy enough to be out here, but he knew he wouldn't be able to sleep. Why the hell had he agreed to go to Fiji? His brain had to be fried from too many hours in Olivia's company. No other explanation popped up. Accepting he wanted time out with her went against everything he strived for. His hands clenched at his sides. What if he liked Olivia even more by the end of the trip? He liked her too much already. Her beauty, her wit, her sense of fun, and her concern for others. He'd pushed her to go away to a place that was all about romance. Romance. A subject he knew nothing about. And didn't want to. That would be like rubbing salt into the wound.

Olivia would be regretting her acceptance of Paul's generous gift. But she would never back down. Not now that others had heard her accept.

Zac sighed unhappily. He was as bad as Olivia. Paul had challenged them both, and he'd fallen for it. Given in to the emotions that had been battering him since he'd arrived at the hotel. To have spent his entire adult life avoiding commitment only to find himself well and truly hooked didn't bear thinking about.

A gust of rain-laden wind slapped them. Olivia pulled her jacket tight across her breasts and folded her arms under them. Her face looked pinched—from cold or from anger at herself for agreeing, he wasn't sure.

Taking her elbow, Zac turned them around. She was shivering. 'Come on. We'll go to my apartment. The weather's about to dump a load of wet stuff and getting soaked doesn't appeal.'

'I should go back to the hotel.' She didn't sound convinced.

'We need to talk about what we've got ourselves into.' Then he might feel happier. Might. 'I've got wine in the chiller. Or there's tea, if you'd prefer.' He also had a huge bed, but doubted he'd get a hug for mentioning that.

'Why didn't you tell Paul no?' she asked when they were in the elevator, heading up to his apartment.

Initially he had. 'Maybe I want to go.'

'Do you? Really?'

While I'm standing here breathing in the floral scent that's you, yes, really. When I see that uncertainty flick through your eyes, yes, I want to spend time with you. When I think about actually scratching my itch, defi-

nitely, yes, but if I remember why I have to move on from you, then a resounding no.

The elevator shook to a halt and the doors glided open. He took her elbow again. 'The idea of going to Fiji, it's growing on me.' His parent's fortieth wedding anniversary was in the first week of July and they were having a party to beat all parties at one of Auckland's top restaurants. Of course he wanted to celebrate with them. Of course he was not invited. 'Yep, getting away has appeal.' He tried to ignore the surprised look on her face and opened the door to his penthouse. 'After you.'

Olivia slipped past him, and walked through to the lounge with its floor-to-ceiling glass wall that allowed an extensive view of Auckland Harbour, the bridge, and closer in the wharves with a collection of large and small sea craft tied up.

He followed, stood next to her, stared out seeing nothing. Why did Olivia unsettle him when no other woman ever had?

'I've never been to the islands,' she said, without looking his way. 'Haven't been anywhere since I was ten, and then it was to Australia with my parents. Mum hates flying.'

'Makes for an uncomfortable trip, I imagine. You haven't inherited that fear?'

Her head moved slowly from side to side. 'Not at all. In fact, I'd like to learn to fly one day.'

'What's holding you back?' It wouldn't be lack of brains or money.

'I have a feeling it would become a passion and what with work and doing up my house there isn't enough spare time to spend hours in the air.' Her reflection in the window showed she was nibbling her lip again.

He didn't like it when she did that. It indicated distress, and he didn't want her to feel distressed. 'Ever thought of cutting back a few hours so you can do some of the things you like?'

Olivia finally looked at him. 'I spent so much time training and working my way to the top that I think I've forgotten there's a whole world out there waiting to be explored, whether through travel or doing things like learning to fly.'

'You're right.' Apart from going sailing whenever he could get a weekend away, he spent most of his time working. 'You said you're enjoying doing up your house. I bought this apartment because the idea of renovations and painting and all the things required to turn a house into a home seemed too huge. It's not a job for one weekend, is it?'

'No, it's a project. But, then, most things I've ever done have been projects.' She frowned. 'That's how I stay in control. Take the house. Next month is bathroom month. The builder's going to gut it and then everything I've chosen goes in and I get to go shopping for all the little bits and pieces, matching the towels with the tile colour, the fittings with the rest of the house.'

Sounded too organised for him. He liked a little disorder, certainly didn't have perfectly matched towels or even dinner sets. Not that he'd gone to the second-hand shop for anything, but he hadn't been hell-bent on getting everything looking like a show home. 'What was last month?'

'My bedroom.' She turned away, and her voice was low as she told him, 'It's cream and rose pink. Very girlie, but I wasn't allowed that when I was growing up so I'm having it now.'

Wow, she'd just mentioned her childhood twice in a short amount of time. Very briefly, sure, but there it was. She hadn't been allowed to pick the colours for her room. Not a big deal maybe, but it could mean there was nothing she'd been allowed to choose. 'I've never seen you wear pink.'

'Rose pink.' Her smile was unexpectedly shy. 'There's a difference. And, no, I can't imagine what patients would think if their surgeon turned up dressed in pink.'

'They'd probably love it.' Taking a step back before he walked into that smile filling him with a longing for something special, he brought everything back to reality. 'Tea or champagne?'

'Have you got camomile?' Her smile had widened into that of a cheeky girl.

He told her, 'Yes, I have,' and laughed at her surprise. 'My mother drinks it.' *On the rare times she's visited.*

'For some reason I didn't think you were close.' She followed him to the kitchen, where she perched on a bar stool at the counter. Crossing her legs showed off a length of thigh where that golden creation that was supposedly a dress rode high.

'We're not.' Mum at least tried to accept he was still her son, while Dad... Forget it.

'You mentioned one brother.' Was that longing in her voice? Hard to tell from her face.

'Mark. He's married with two kids. I only get to see them at Christmas and birthdays.'

Olivia picked at an invisible spot on the counter. 'That's incredibly sad.'

'Yep.' He made himself busy getting mugs from the cupboard and teabags from the pantry.

She lifted her head and locked her blue eyes on him, suddenly back to being in control. 'Think I'll head back to the hotel. I don't really want tea. Or anything.' She slipped off the stool and turned towards the doorway. 'Good night, Zac.'

With little thought he reached for her, caught her wrist and gently tugged her close. With a finger under her chin he tilted her head back so he could gaze down into her eyes. And felt his head spinning with wanting her.

Olivia's eyes widened and her chin rose further as her mouth opened slightly.

Zac was lost. Any resistance or logical thinking disappeared as he leaned closer to place his mouth over hers. As he tasted her, the heat and need he'd kept tamped down most of the night exploded into a rainbow of hot colours. Olivia. She was in his arms, her mouth on his, her tongue dancing with his. Olivia.

Slim arms wound around his neck, pulling his body closer to hers. He felt her rise onto tiptoe, knew the moment when her hips pressed against his obvious desire. Those breasts he'd been fantasising about all night flattened against his chest, turning him into a molten pool of need. His hands spread around her waist to lift her onto the stool, where she immediately wrapped her legs around his thighs.

This is what I've missed so damned much. We are fire on fire. Feeding each other. Consuming the oxygen.

She tasted wonderful, bringing more erotic memories back to him. Making new ones.

Lifting his mouth, he began trailing kisses over her jaw, down her neckline, on towards her deep cleavage. When she whimpered he continued while lifting his gaze to her face, where he recognised the same fiery awakening racing along his veins.

Her fingers kneaded his scalp as she pushed her breasts higher to give him more access with his tongue.

She wasn't wearing a bra. Of course she wasn't. That dress had clung to every curve and outlined her shape perfectly; including her breasts, those peaks now hard against his mouth and hand.

Zac growled as he licked her, tasted her skin, her nipple. A gentle bite had her arching her back and tipping her head so that her hair fell like a waterfall behind her. And he lost himself, tasting, touching, rubbing.

'It's been so long,' she murmured in a low voice that spelt sex. Her hands fumbled with the buttons of his shirt, finally pushed it open, and then her palms were on his skin, smoothing and teasing as only Olivia could do.

The memories that he'd lived on for all those long months apart rapidly became reality. He hadn't enhanced any of them. This was how it had been between them. Then his belt was loose, the zip being tugged downward, and... *Oh, hell.* Her soft hand was wrapped around him, sliding down, up, and down again. *Oh, hell.* There was nothing quite like making out with this woman. She knew the buttons to push, remembered what he most enjoyed, and if she wasn't careful would have him coming long before he'd pleasured her.

That wasn't happening. Zac wrapped his arms around her and carried her quickly down the hall to his bedroom and the super-king-sized bed she had yet to try out. Toeing his shoes off, he knelt on the bed and leaned forward with Olivia still in his arms so that he was covering her before she could move. 'Your turn.'

'I'm ready,' she croaked.

'I haven't touched you yet.' But, then, often he hadn't had to. All part of that explosiveness that had been them.

'Don't, if you want this to last more than the next three seconds.'

Now, there was a challenge. Pushing her dress up over her thighs, Zac slipped down to find her core with his tongue. The moment he tasted her she jolted like she'd been zapped with an electrical current.

Her hands gripped his head, holding him there. Not that he'd been going anywhere else until he had her rocking against him.

'Zac!' she cried when he licked her. 'Zachary...' As he pushed a finger inside.

Her hips lifted, her fingers pressed into his scalp, and she was crying out his name. Over and over as her body convulsed under him.

Reaching for the top drawer of his bedside table, he grabbed a condom and tore the packet open with his teeth. A small, warm hand whipped the condom from his fingers. 'Let me.'

Then he was lying on his back, unsure how she'd managed to flip him so effortlessly. She straddled his thighs and, achingly slowly, slid the condom onto his erection.

Placing his hands on her waist, he lifted her over him and lowered her to cover him, took him inside to her moist, hot centre.

'Zac!' She screamed his name.

He hadn't forgotten she was a screamer but it still hit him hard, stirred him and had him pushing further into her.

It was never going to take long, he was that hot for her, had been wanting this from the moment he'd seen her leaning against that counter in the hotel reception. When she put her hand behind to squeeze him he was gone. Over. Finished. One final thrust and Olivia cried out and fell over his chest, gasping for air, her skin slick with sweat and her body trembling against his.

As she lay sprawled across him, he spread his hands across her back, stared up at the barely illuminated ceiling and smiled. Everything was in place in his world. Olivia was in his bed. They'd shared the mind-blowing sex he knew only with her. Everything was perfect. His itch was being appeased.

Or would be when they did it again, just as soon as he got his breath back.

CHAPTER SIX

ZAC HAD NO idea what the time was when he rolled over and reached out for Olivia, only to come up empty-handed. 'Olivia?' He sat up and stared around. His heart thumped hard. Not again.

'I'm here.' Her voice came from the en suite bathroom.

Phew. He dropped back. Something clattered in the hand basin, and Olivia swore. 'You okay in there?' he called.

Silence.

'Olivia? Are you all right?' His gut started to tighten.

'I'm making sure I can walk past the hotel receptionist without looking like I've been…um, doing what I've been doing.'

'You're heading over the road?' Now he was on full alert. Swinging his legs over the side of the bed, he stood. 'What's wrong with staying the rest of the night? You and I don't usually settle for once.'

'Don't do this, Zac.' She stepped into the room, but kept her distance. 'We've got to stop before we get carried away.'

As the cold reality of her words hit him he pulled his head back, glared down at her. 'Why? We are willing, consenting adults, not two teenagers who have to go home to Mum and Dad looking guilty.' Hopefully she didn't hear the anger her rejection made him feel. Again. And the pain because she was right.

'I'm sorry.' Her eyes were brimming with tears. 'I shouldn't have got so carried away.'

A gut-buster, that statement. 'We got carried away, sweetheart. We.' He shoved a hand through his hair, trying to figure out what had happened to cause her to haul on the brakes. He should be grateful. He'd hoped to sooth his need, not crank it wide-open. How wrong could a bloke be?

'Exactly. We didn't stop to think about what we were doing. Not for a moment.' Her back was straight, her shoulders tight, but her chin wobbled as she said, 'Which is why I can't go to Fiji with you.'

'You're changing your mind?' Of course she was. For some reason he didn't feel happy. He'd enjoyed being with her tonight. It had been like finding something precious after a long search. He could barely look at her and not reach for her again. She might've put the brakes on but it would take a tank of icy water to cool his ardour and return his out-of-whack heart rate to normal.

In the doorway she hesitated, turned around to look at him, sorrow leaking out of those baby blues. 'Yes, Zac, I am. Going on holiday together would only exacerbate the situation. I can't have another affair with you. It's too casual, and anything more is impossible for me.'

He stood rooted to the floor, unable to ignore the sharp pain her statement caused yet knowing she was stronger than him. The itch had gone beyond scratchy, was now an open wound that needed healing. Olivia was the cure but, as she'd so clearly pointed out, that wasn't about to happen.

Moments later his main door clicked shut, presumably behind her, and still he stood transfixed. For a moment earlier on, when they'd been sated with sex, he thought he'd found that untouchable thing he'd been looking for in his dreams and pushing away when he was wide-awake. Hell, he'd felt as though he'd connected with Olivia in a way he'd never connected with another human being in his life. Sure, they'd had sex without any preamble, as they'd always done, but there'd been more depth to their liaison. He'd made love to the woman of his dreams. Literally.

Which made Olivia heading back to her hotel room absolutely right. Unlike him, she had a handle on their situation. Where was his gratitude?

Zac's phone vibrated its way across the bedside table. 'Hello?' Had Olivia had a change of heart?

'It's North Shore Emergency Unit, Dr Wright. We've got a situation.'

Not Olivia. Guess it wasn't his night. 'Tell me,' he sighed.

'A bus full of rowers returning to Whangarei went off the road an hour out of the city. There are many casualties so we're ringing round everyone. Can you come in?'

'On my way.' It wasn't as though he'd been sleeping. A certain woman had taken up residence in his skull, refusing to let him drop off to sleep even when his body was craving rest.

'Kelly Devlin, nineteen-year-old rower, fractured tibia,' the ED registrar told Zac within moments of him striding into the chaotic department.

Zac studied the X-rays on the light box. 'She needs a rod insertion,' he decided, and went to talk to his patient.

Kelly glared at him. 'I'm a national rowing champion, Doctor. I can't have a broken leg.'

Zac's heart went out to her. 'You have. I'm sorry.'

'Does that mean the end of my career?'

'First I'll explain what I'm going to do to help you.' He sat on the edge of her bed. 'I've seen the X-rays and your left tibia is fractured in two places. To allow the bone to heal without too much added stress I'm going to put a titanium rod down the centre of the bone. There will be screws to hold it in place while you heal.' He kept the details scant. He knew from experience that too much information at this stage usually confused the patient and added to their distress.

'Will I be competitive again?' the girl demanded.

'That will take a lot of work on your part, but I don't see why not.' When disbelief stared him in the eye, he added, 'You're a champion rower so you know what it's like to work your butt off to get where you want to be. This will be harder. Your muscles will need strengthening and the bone will require time to knit.' He hoped he wasn't misleading Kelly. 'You may have to compensate in some way for the damaged leg, but we won't know for sure until further down the track.'

Tears slid down her cheeks. 'You're honest, but I don't have to like what you're telling me. It's going to be painful for a while, isn't it?'

'You'll have painkillers.' Bone pain. Not good. 'A physiotherapist will have you working on that leg when I think you're ready.'

'When are you operating?'

'As soon as I get things sorted a nurse will come and get you ready for Theatre.' He stood up. 'I'll see you in there. Have your family been told about the accident?'

'Mum and Dad are on their way from Whangarei,

but I don't want to wait. If I've had surgery before they arrive it'll be easier on them.' She shifted on the bed and cried out as pain jagged her.

'Take it easy. Try to stay as still as possible. You'll soon be given a pre-anaesthetic drug that will make you feel drowsy and dull your senses a little.' Zac nodded at the nurse on the other side of the bed. 'I'll talk to the anaesthetist now, get everything under way.'

As he headed out of the ED to arrange everything Zac rubbed the back of his neck. What a night.

'Morning, everyone. Sorry I'm late. Forgot to set my alarm.' Olivia slid into the only vacant chair at the table in the hotel dining room where she was having a late brunch with Andy and his family, Maxine and Brent Sutherland, who were Andy's close friends, and Zac.

'Have a late night?' Zac asked.

She scowled at him. 'Something like that.'

He told her, 'I've been in surgery.'

'Already? Were you on call?' He'd have mentioned it, wouldn't he?

'A bus went over the bank near Waiwera. The hospital needed orthopaedic surgeons in a hurry.'

'Why was a bus travelling through the night?' she asked.

'Taking rowers home from the nationals down south.'

'Coffee or tea?' A waitress hovered with the brunch menu.

'We've all ordered,' Zac informed her.

'The kitchen will make sure your meal comes out with the others,' the waitress said. 'Drink?'

Yes, yes, yes. Give me a moment. Olivia took the proffered menu. 'A pot of English Breakfast tea, thank you.'

A quick read of the list of tasty dishes on offer. 'Pancakes with bacon and banana, and lots of maple syrup.'

When she turned to find Zac watching her with a soft smile on those adorable lips she snapped, 'What?'

'Pancakes and syrup? I thought you'd be a muesli and fruit girl.'

She was. Always. But this morning her usually strict control over her diet had gone the same place any control seemed to go when Zac was around—out west somewhere beyond the hills. 'Thought I'd spoil myself.' She looked around the table at her friends. Zac's friends too, don't forget. 'Did everyone enjoy last night?'

'You have to ask?' Maxine asked with a grin. 'The band kept playing until one and only stopped because the hotel management asked them to.'

'The dinner was amazing,' Brent added.

Olivia looked at the boys sitting quietly opposite her. 'Did you all have fun too?'

'Yeah. But Mum made us go to our room early. I liked dancing,' the oldest said.

'Your mum's mean.' Andy grinned tiredly. Now that the excitement of the night before had worn off he looked as though he had little energy left.

'It's part of the job description,' Zac added.

'That was a generous gift from Paul,' Maxine chipped in. 'I'm assuming you're both going to take it up. I mean, who wouldn't go to a luxury island in Fiji, all expenses paid? I know I would.'

'Does everyone know?' Olivia shivered. No way would she go after how things had played out last night in Zac's apartment. Nearly a week sharing a bure with Zac would make a joke of her self-control. Remaining impervious to Zac's charm would be impossible. As she'd already proved. 'I don't think I'll be going.'

Unfortunately her eyes drifted to the right and locked with Zac's.

'If that's what you want.'

She wasn't sure about it being what she wanted, but she knew it was how it had to be for her sanity. Amidst exclamations from just about everyone else at the table Olivia told Zac quietly, for his ears only, 'It's for the best.'

'Yours, or mine?' Why the disappointment? Surely he hadn't thought they'd be having a five-day sex fest? Though, if she was being truthful with herself, he had good reason to think that, given how quickly they'd leapt into each other's arms last night.

'Ours.' A picture of blue sea and coconut palms crossed her mind. Going to Fiji would be marvellous. That lump at the bottom of her stomach was her disappointment. It was a great opportunity and she was reneging on it.

'Last night you accepted.' Zac's words arrowed to the core of her concern.

'I did.' She'd be letting Paul down after he'd done something so generous. She wasn't used to people doing things like that for her. She had a feeling she'd also let Zac down. Would he want to go alone? Or could he take someone else with him? Jealousy raised its ugly head. She didn't want Zac going to the tropical island with another woman. If he was going she wanted to be the one at his side. In his arms. Gulp. *Make up your mind. What do you want with Zac?*

She wanted Zac in her life. But to follow up on that would be dangerous. What if they did get close; moved in together? How long would that last? When her mother acted once too often with the mess Olivia was used to dealing with, would Zac walk? If she had a month like she'd had in February, when she'd had so much work she'd all but lived in the hospital for four weeks, would he begrudge the time he didn't have with her and leave? There'd only been one man in her life she'd loved unconditionally—her father—and he'd deserted her. She doubted her ability to cope with anyone else doing that to her.

Her tea arrived and she concentrated on pouring, tried hard to ignore the dilemma going on in her head.

But Zac didn't seem to have any problem continuing the conversation. 'I take it this is because of what happened in my apartment?' He leaned closer so only she could hear him.

Unfortunately his movement brought that heady smell that defined him closer to her nostrils. There was no avoiding the scent, or the challenge in his eyes. 'We wouldn't be able to go the distance without touching each other.'

'Is that what you want?' Disbelief darkened his eyes, deepened his voice. Who could blame him? Last night she hadn't mucked around about getting into the sack with him. He asked, 'Seriously?

No, she wanted to spend the whole time in bed with him. That was the problem. 'It's what I need.'

Zac sat back, leaning away from her, his gaze fixed on her as though he hoped to see inside her skull and read her mind. 'I should be glad you're saying no, but there's one fabulous holiday going begging. Until Paul pointed it out I hadn't realised how much I could do with a break. Fiji would be perfect.'

Olivia said, 'You can still go.'

'Not much fun alone,' he said softly.

'Apply the pressure, why don't you?'

'Yep.'

'Not happening,' she muttered. Lifting her cup, Olivia tried to concentrate on what the others were talking about. When the meals arrived she joined in the conversation, relieved that the subject of Fiji had been dropped. But all the while that picture of the sea and coconut palms remained at the forefront of her mind, with Zac firmly in the middle.

Her phone rang just as everyone was getting up from the table to go their separate ways.

'Olivia, it's Hugo. I'm sorry to disturb your weekend when I said I'd cover for you, but I'm concerned about Anna Seddon.'

Alarm made her voice sharp. 'What's up?' Anna was a healthy woman who shouldn't be having any post-op complications.

'Medically she's fine. Her obs couldn't be better, she slept well until four this morning. But she's having a meltdown about the operation. I've tried talking to her but I'm a mere male and have no idea what it's like to have my breasts removed.' Hugo sighed. 'She's right, of course.'

'Of all the people I've done that procedure for I'd never have thought Anna would break up about it. She's been so pragmatic.' Olivia echoed Hugo's sigh. 'Is her husband with her?'

'Yes, and looking lost. She keeps yelling at him to go away. He doesn't know how to help her either.'

And I can? She had to try. She'd told Anna she'd be there for her throughout this difficult time, and she had meant it. 'I'll come over now.' She dropped her phone into her handbag and turned to face everyone. 'Thanks for the catch-up, guys. I've got to go.'

Maxine stepped up to give her a hug. 'Don't take

so long next time. I want to hear all the details about your trip to Fiji.'

'There won't be any. I'm not going.' She tried to free herself from Maxine's arms and failed.

'Go. It would be good for you.'

Maxine dropped her arms to her sides and Olivia stepped back.

'You might be surprised.'

Olivia couldn't help herself: she glanced across at the man in question. His familiar face snatched at her heart. Talking animatedly with the others, he appeared relaxed and comfortable in his own skin. Then he looked over at her and winked. Caught. He'd been aware of her scrutiny all along. Like they were in tune with each other, which was nonsense. They'd never been like that. Except when it came to sex. But there was nothing sexual about that wink. It had been more a 'Hey, girl' gesture. Friendly and caring, not deep and loving or hot and demanding. But it had been…? Nice? Yes, nice.

Turning back to Maxine, she said, 'I'd better run. A patient needs me.'

'You have to be somewhere in a hurry?' Zac strode alongside her as she raced for the lobby and the elevators, keen to get away before anyone else brought up the subject of that trip away with Zac.

'The hospital. I did a double mastectomy and implant yesterday morning and apparently my patient is losing it big time this morning.'

'That's a biggie for any woman to deal with.'

'She's been so brave all the way through discussions about the operation and what size implants she'd like. She's dealt with her family's history of breast cancer matter-of-factly, and accepted she didn't have a lot of

choice if she wanted longevity. Guess it had to catch
up with her some time.'

'Has she got good support from her family?' Zac
asked as he pressed the up button for the elevator.

'Yes, very good.' Olivia drew a breath. Only yesterday she'd been saying to the Theatre staff how Anna's
husband was a hero in her book. Yep, and she'd had
thoughts about the man next to her being a hero too.

'You want me to get your car out of the basement?
Save you some minutes?'

She stared at Zac. 'I forgot. I need to order a taxi.
My car's in the hospital car park with a flat battery. I
didn't have time to phone a service man yesterday.' She
made to head for the concierge only to be stopped by
Zac's hand on her arm.

'I'll be waiting in my car out the front when you're
ready.' He nudged her forward into the elevator. 'It'll
only take a couple of minutes to get it.'

*But I don't want to sit in a car with you, breathing
your smell, feeling your heat, wishing I could go away
with you.* 'A taxi will be fine.' She was talking to the
closing doors, Zac already halfway across the lobby.
She'd lost that round. There'd been determination in the
set of his shoulders and the length of his quick strides
taking him out of the hotel. He'd be ready for her the
moment she emerged from the revolving door of the
hotel.

Nice.

Leaning back against the wall, Olivia smiled despite her misgivings. She'd have to come up with a better word than 'nice'. Zac was more than nice, and his
gestures were kind and caring. All good, all sounding
bland for a man who was anything but. 'Hot' used to be
her word for him and, yes, he was still that.

But now? Now he was a mixed bag of emotions and characteristics she hadn't taken the time to notice before. This Zac was intriguing. She wanted to know more about him. Hell, she wanted to know everything.

As the elevator pinged at her floor she knew she had to walk away from him, because the more she learned about Zac the harder it became to remain aloof. Her emotions were getting involved, putting her heart in turmoil, and that was a no-go zone.

CHAPTER SEVEN

'I AM SO SORRY.' Anna Seddon sniffed, and snatched up a handful of tissues to blow her nose. 'I know it's your weekend off. Hugo shouldn't have called you.'

Olivia sat on the edge of the bed and shook her head at her patient. 'It's not a problem. I'd have been annoyed if he hadn't. What started this off? What's distressed you this morning?'

'I took a look under the gown and saw where my breasts used to be. It's horrible there. The new ones don't look right even wrapped in bandages. I know you said to wait, but I had to see.' Anna slashed at fresh tears spilling down her cheeks. 'Nothing looks normal. The implants are different, ugly, not me, and the scars are bright red. I shouldn't have done this. I should've taken a chance I wouldn't get cancer.'

Olivia waited until Anna ran out of steam, then took her hand. 'You've had a shock. No amount of explaining could've prepared you.' Which was why she asked patients to wait until she was there before they looked at the results of their surgery. 'Remember, I said that your breast implants were going to look and feel strange. They're not natural, like your real breasts were, and we have yet to bring them up to full size. This will take time as we can't pump them full of saline instantly. It's a gradual process, giving your skin time to stretch and accommodate the implants.'

'You told me that, but I saw them and freaked out,' Anna whispered. 'You must think I'm a total head case.'

'Not at all. You've just had your breasts removed when as far as we know there's nothing wrong with them. You're not dealing with the fear of knowing you've already got cancer. Instead, breast cancer is a real possibility for you, so you're working ahead of things. Of course it's a shock and very different from other situations.'

'I know you went over this more than once. I thought I understood how I'd feel, and that the fact I was doing it to be there for my kids and Duncan would override every other emotion. I was wrong.' At the mention of her husband tears began pouring down her face again.

'You're a woman, first and foremost. Our breasts help define us. When we're young we can't wait for them to start growing and then it's what size will they be? Will they be sexy? They're also about nurturing our babies. You've done something very brave. Don't ever think you're not as feminine as you were before yesterday because you are. You've got a lovely figure, a pretty face and a heart of gold. Not to mention a family who adores you. Especially that husband of yours.'

A shadow of a smile lightened Anna's mouth through the deluge of tears. 'Duncan's something, isn't he?'

'He's a hero.' There, she'd said it again. What was it with her that she kept coming up with that word? It wasn't as though she believed in heroes. *But you want to. You want one of your own.*

'You think?' Anna asked, a twinkle slowly lightening her sad eyes and easing her tears.

'I know.' She stood up. 'In fact, there's a hero out

in the waiting room. I'll go tell him you're busting to see him.'

'What will he say when he sees my false breasts?' There was a hitch in Anna's voice and fear in her eyes.

'I bet he tells you he loves you.' Lucky woman. *What was it like to have a man to love you, to say those precious three words to you?* Olivia had never known and wondered if she ever would. It must be the most precious thing—love, unconditional and everlasting. When she walked into the waiting room she found Zac talking rugby to Anna Seddon's husband as though he'd known him for ever.

Her heart did a funny little jig. Zac. Sexy Zac was doing nothing more than yakking to a stranger who was trying to cope with his wife's unenviable situation, and yet he looked…like everything she'd thought she might want in a man, in her man. Her hero.

Get out of here. Where had that come from? Yeah, sure, yesterday when she'd called Duncan a hero it had been Zac's face flitting across her mind, but Zac? Hero? Why would she even think that? What had he done for her to think so?

She'd dumped him and he'd sent her beautiful flowers.

He'd driven her here this morning and taken her keys to get her car battery sorted.

He'd turned up to help yesterday afternoon when everything had been turning to custard.

He'd never once been rude to her, or made fun of her need to keep herself to herself, or told her to stop being so much in control of just about everything she touched.

Did any or all of those things make a man a hero? Didn't heroes slay dragons? She still had dragons, but Zac didn't know about them because she'd never shown that weakness to him. It wasn't as though he could make everything right for her, even if he was aware of her screwed-up family life.

'CC, you're daydreaming.' Zac was smiling at her, his head at an angle that suggested he wanted to know exactly what was on her mind.

Thank goodness she wasn't the type to blush. The absolute last thing Zac needed to know was what she'd been thinking. 'I don't daydream.'

'Then you're missing out on a lot of fun.'

'How's Anna?' There was a load of worry in Duncan's short question.

'Wanting to see her man.' Olivia moved closer. 'She's got past that little meltdown but, Duncan, you need to be prepared for more episodes. I'm not saying Anna's going to fall apart on you long term, but she's facing reality now, whereas before surgery it was still an unknown. It's scary for her.' She continued, 'She's afraid you won't be able to cope when you see her breasts. It's natural to feel that way, but it's how you handle the situation that's going to make the difference.'

'I'll tell you this for nothing. I don't care about scars and a change in her shape. I love that woman and think she's the bravest person I've ever met.' Duncan touched the corner of one eye with a forefinger.

'I think Anna's a lucky woman.' Olivia swallowed the sudden lump in her throat. 'Go tell her exactly what you just said.'

'She's not going to throw her water bottle at me or tell me to go away for ever?' Duncan was deadly serious.

'I doubt it, unless it's because you've taken so long to get along to her room since I said I was coming to find you.' Anna shouldn't have thrown anything—it would hurt her wounds and might pull some stitches. Something to check up on when she examined her later. She hadn't wanted to have Anna expose herself for an exam when she'd been so upset, and had figured that as all the obs were fine it didn't matter if they waited before doing that.

Dropping into the seat Duncan had vacated, she stared at the toes of her boots. And yawned.

Zac chuckled. 'Want to grab a coffee while we wait for the battery man? He's about twenty minutes away and we could both do with something to keep us awake.'

'Hospital coffee will be a comedown after that fabulous brunch.'

'Nothing like a reality check.'

Reality. Of course. 'You don't need to hang around. You've got a perfectly good vehicle downstairs. I can visit patients while I wait.'

'You don't want to share crap coffee with me?' His grin set butterflies flapping in her tummy. 'Anyway, the guy's got my number, not yours.'

'I hate it when you gloat.' She laughed tiredly. 'Disgusting coffee it is.' Along with great company. All in all, not a bad way to continue her morning.

Olivia's bubble burst quickly.

Zac directed her to a corner table as far away as possible from the few staff and visitors using the cafeteria, ordered long blacks for them both, and dropped onto the chair opposite her. 'I've talked to my practice manager so she can arrange for my days off when we go to Fiji. The hospital roster is easy to fix, with Paul offering to cover for me.'

The man didn't muck about. He must've been on the phone the moment she'd clambered out of his four-wheel drive in the hospital garage; ordering a battery, sorting his week off.

She sighed. 'I thought I said I wasn't going.' He had to be deaf as well as organised.

'You did.'

'So you *are* planning on going alone.'

'Nope.' Zac leaned back as a girl placed two over-full coffee cups on the table and took away their order number. 'I want you to come with me.'

So do I. 'No.'

Those eyes that matched the coffee in colour locked onto her. 'Are you telling *me* no? Or yourself, Olivia?'

'We'd probably end up hating each other.'

'Somehow I don't think so.' Shock widened his eyes. So he hadn't thought it through. 'But we won't know if we don't try.'

What was this about? Zac had made it clear he'd only been interested in sex last time round. Her hands were back in her lap, her fingers aching with the tightness of her grip. 'Is this so you can then walk away with no regrets? Did I finish it too soon last time?'

Now his gaze dropped away. He leaned far back and draped one arm over the top of the chair next to him. His eyes cruised the cafeteria before returning to her, a guarded expression covering his face. 'I've learned more about you in the last twenty-four hours than I ever did in those eight weeks last year.'

'Then you're probably up to speed and there's nothing more to find out.'

Zac stared at her. 'You're selling yourself short.'

To hell with the coffee. Pushing up from the table, she aimed for a moderate tone. 'No, I am not. What you see is what you get, and as for Fiji, you get nothing. I'm not going.' *But I want to. Really, really want to.*

Of course he followed her. He was persistent if nothing else. Unlike last time. 'Rethink that, Olivia. We don't have to live in each other's pockets while we're there, but it would be fun to lie in the sun together, to share a meal under the stars.'

The problem was that if she lay on the beach in her bikini beside Zac in his swimming shorts they would end up having sex. Not that doing so didn't appeal. Of course it did. Her mouth watered, thinking about it. But she'd made up her mind the day she'd walked out on him that they weren't going anywhere with their relationship because she couldn't afford to get her heart broken. Neither had she wanted to break his—if it was even up for grabs.

Zac pulled his phone from his pocket and read a message. 'Your battery's nearly here.'

'Good. Thanks for arranging it.' She didn't know why she felt small and mean, only knew she was floundering, fighting between going with him on that trip and staying away from temptation. She was looking out for herself, something she'd always done. Her mother had never put her daughter before herself, never would. She gasped. That meant she was the same as her mother. Putting her determination to remain alone before anyone, anything else. *But… But I'm doing it for a good reason. Dad left Mum because she'd worn him down, tossed his love back in his face again and again. I'm not doing that to a man I might fall in love with.*

A hand on her elbow directed her to the elevator. Seemed that Zac was always taking her to the lift. 'Five days of sunshine and no patients. Sounds wonderful to me.'

Ain't that the truth?

At least Olivia hadn't questioned why he was so ada-mant they should go to Fiji together. He should be grate-ful she was refusing to go, but the thought of being alone when he should be celebrating with his family grated. A distraction was needed and Olivia would cer-tainly be that.

But, more than that, it was time to start changing from being reactive to his family's attitude to becoming proactive in sorting out what he wanted for his future— starting with taking time off from his heavy work sched-ule to have some fun. Hell. When was the last time he'd done that? Nothing came to mind except the hours he'd snatched to be with Olivia eighteen months ago.

The sound of squealing tyres filled the basement ga-rage as they exited the elevator on the way to the out-side car park. The smell of burning rubber filled his nostrils. 'What the hell?'

A nearly new, upmarket car raced past them. At the end of the lane it spun left, the rear wheels sliding out of control. Just when impact with parked vehicles seemed imminent the driver got the car under control.

Zac pushed Olivia back against the now closed el-evator doors, tugged his phone from his pocket to call Security, and cursed. There was no signal down here. 'The driver looked very young. How'd he get in?'

The garage and car park were reserved for medi-cal personnel and accessed with a swipe card. The car flew past them again as Zac looked around for a wall phone. Spying one by the stairwell door, he changed direction, only to spin around when he heard an almighty thump, followed by a metallic crashing sound. Then ominous silence.

'He's hit someone and then slammed into a vehicle!' Olivia began running in the direction of the crashed car.

Zac raced alongside her. 'We need someone down here, taking charge of that kid.' A boy looking about fifteen staggered out of the car, looking shocked and bewildered.

'Where did she come from?' he squawked as they reached him.

Zac's hands clenched as he saw a woman in blue scrubs sprawled across the concrete, a pool of blood already beginning to form by her head. 'What the hell were you doing?' Zac shouted at the kid as he dropped down to his knees beside the unmoving woman.

'Hey, steady.' Olivia reached across from the other side of the woman to grip his arm. Shaking her head at him, she said, 'This nurse needs our undivided attention.'

'You're right,' he ground through gritted teeth. 'Kid, get on that phone by the elevator and get help down here fast.'

Without a word the youth was gone, and Zac could only hope he was running for the phone.

Zac felt for a pulse, and sighed with relief.

Olivia was carefully feeling the nurse's head. 'Amelia, can you hear me?'

A low groan was the only answer she got.

'Amelia, you've been in an accident. There are two doctors with you and we're going to check your injuries.'

'How much do you think she's heard?' Zac wondered aloud.

Olivia shrugged. 'We can't be sure anything we say registers.'

'You know her?' Zac noted the odd angle of the

nurse's legs and checked for bleeding in case a blood vessel had been torn. 'No major swelling indicating internal bleeding.'

'I can read,' Olivia muttered.

The name badge. Duh. Left his brain behind this morning, had he? With gentle movements he began assessing her hips and thighs for fractures. 'Broken femur for starters. This knee has taken a thump too.' His fingers worked over the kneecap. 'Smashed, I'd say.'

Their patient groaned again and lifted an arm a small way off the ground.

Zac quickly caught her, and gently pressed her arm down by her side. 'Amelia, try not to move.'

One eye opened, shut again.

'At least she's responding,' he said.

'Oh, my God. What's happened?' A man loomed over them.

Zac told him, 'An out-of-control car hit her.'

The newcomer said, 'I'm in Admin, but I can get help if you tell me what you need.'

'Get us the emergency equipment and a bed. I told the driver to ring upstairs but you're part of this hospital, you'll know exactly who to speak to,' Zac told him. Who knew if the boy had done as he'd said or taken a hike before everyone turned up and started pointing fingers?

Olivia was speaking quietly. 'We've got a soft cranial injury, probably from impacting with the concrete. Left ear's torn.'

Zac added to the list of injuries. 'At least her chest appears to have dodged a bullet.' His fingers were gently working over Amelia's ribs. 'The car would've hit her in the lower body.' What had that kid been thinking, doing wheelies in here? He hadn't looked old enough to know how to drive. *Who are you to ask? You were eighteen and still got it wrong.*

'On my way.' The admin man nodded at the vehicle parked with its nose caught in the side panel of a sedan. 'That the car? It's Maxine Sutherland's.'

Olivia's head shot up, horror in her eyes, but all she said was, 'Can you run? This woman needs urgent help.'

With the man gone, Zac said, 'Maxine must've left the car unlocked, unless...' Had it been Maxine and Brent's son driving? Shock rocked through Zac. No parent ever wanted to deal with something like this. He knew. He'd done it to his brother and parents, with dire consequences. They'd never forgiven him, blaming him for not looking out for his younger brother. Like they'd ever been there for either of their sons. But every time Zac saw his brother and that blasted wheelchair the guilt crunched his insides. Zac's remorse would never go away, and was stronger than anything anyone else could lay on him.

'Zac? You okay?' A gentle hand touched his cheek.

His chest rose as he dragged in a lungful of air. 'Yes.' *No.* Now wasn't the time to explain. If ever there was a right time. He tried to straighten Amelia's right leg. 'Her knee is also dislocated.' He had to know. 'Do you think the kid is Maxine and Brent's boy?'

Distress blinked out at him from Olivia's hyacinth eyes. 'No. Couldn't be.' Her bottom lip trembled even as the truth pushed aside her automatic denial. 'How dreadful for them if he is.'

'He was in here, and only card holders have access.'

They were interrupted by the sound of people running and an emergency trolley laden with everything they needed being pushed at a fast pace between the cars. Guess the kid had fronted up for help.

As Olivia explained to the ED staff what had happened and her assessment of Amelia's injuries, the anger Zac had put on the back burner roared to life. 'That boy really has made a mess of things for her.' Zac was equally worried for the lad. *His* life had changed for ever. 'Where is he, anyway?'

'Probably safer away from you.' Olivia came to stand beside him and reached for his hand. 'Calm down, Zac. You're not helping an already tricky situation. I know he's done wrong but let's leave that to others while we help with the medical side of things.'

The last thing Zac wanted was Olivia telling him what to do. It took a moment for it to register in the red haze of his brain that he had an excuse to put distance between them. 'The battery guy. I'll go and wait for him at the gate.' He needed to get away from what had happened before he blew a gasket. Amelia was getting all the attention she needed from Olivia and the ED doctor, while his attitude wasn't helping anyone. He stomped off before Olivia could say anything more.

But not before he saw the shock in those beautiful eyes. Yes, he had his secrets, just as he suspected she had hers. Secrets neither of them wanted to share. His definitely held him back from having a complete and fulfilling life. Was it the same with Olivia? Could that be why she'd walked out on their affair? She hadn't wanted to keep going in case they grew close?

There was nothing for it. They had to take that trip. Time together, talking, relaxing, getting to know each other on a whole new level, was becoming imperative.

Which really meant he should sign up for every orthopaedic surgery coming up at his clinic for the next six months.

CHAPTER EIGHT

OLIVIA POURED BOILING water over the tea leaves. Earl Grey Blue Star. 'Bliss.' She sniffed the air.

Every bone in her body ached with weariness. Her head pounded, her muscles drooped, and it felt as if there was grit in her eyes. The long soak in a very hot shower probably hadn't woken her up at all. Seven o'clock on Saturday night and she couldn't wait to crawl into bed. How pathetic could she get?

Her stomach was crying out to be fed. She hadn't eaten since brunch—the incident in the hospital garage and the resulting investigation by the traffic police had taken up a lot of the day. The pizza she'd ordered would arrive at the front door within the hour. She licked her lips in anticipation and tasted tea.

Her sitting room felt cosy, and lounging in pyjamas and a baggy sweatshirt in front of the fire she'd lit earlier felt decadent. A rare treat to be so sloppily dressed, and she'd die if anyone but the pizza delivery girl saw her in this state.

Right now a holiday would be perfect. *There's one on offer.* Had she been too hasty turning it down? *Not going to think about it.*

Picking up the remote, she turned on the TV, volume low, and flicked through the channels. Nothing interested her, not even the spunky guy showing how to swing a golf club. Not that sport of any kind interested her. It required energy she didn't like expending getting sweaty.

At the moment the most energetic she wanted to be was lying on a beach, getting a tan. Fiji would do that every time. She sighed. Fiji with Zac? What was wrong with her? She should be grabbing those tickets and packing her bag.

The doorbell rang loud in the quiet house. Someone out there must be looking out for her because that pizza was early. She went to get her dinner.

'Hi, Olivia. I hope you don't mind me dropping by.'

'Zac.' Her stomach growled while her heart lifted.

'Is that a good "Zac", or a go away "Zac"?'

'Take your pick.' She stepped back, opening the door wide.

Zac walked in quickly, as though afraid she'd change her mind.

She probably would've if she'd had the energy to think about the consequences of letting him into her home. 'Along here.' She led him into the sitting room.

When his gaze landed on her tea he asked, 'Got anything stronger? Scotch on the rocks?' He sank onto the couch and stared into the fire.

'Sure.' That was one spirit she did have, kept for her delightful elderly neighbour who liked an occasional tipple when he dropped in after a lonely day at home.

Returning with a glass, ice and whisky, Olivia placed everything on the coffee table she'd spent weeks sanding and varnishing to make it beautiful. Taking her mug to the other end of the couch, she sat with her feet tucked under her bottom and flicked glances at her visitor.

Something was going on. He'd been furious when

Amelia had been knocked down by that car. No, as he'd told her angrily, it had been the boy who'd banged the car into Amelia. The car was not at fault. Couldn't argue with that.

His anger had been more than she'd have expected, but there hadn't been an opportunity to talk to him about it. When they'd realised it might've been their colleagues' son doing wheelies in the garage Zac had turned pale and charged outside to let the battery guy into the car park. Later she'd seen him standing beside her car, hands on hips, staring up at the rain-laden sky, impervious to everything going on around him. When he'd joined her and the police, he'd gained some control over his emotions but hadn't been able to look her in the eye. After they'd finished telling the cops what little they'd seen Zac had been quick to drive away, leaving her none the wiser about what had been going on. Now here he was, looking badly in need of some quiet time and a big hug.

She'd give him the quiet time by waiting until he was ready to talk, but she'd hold back on the hug in case she'd read him wrong and he took it as more than she intended.

Zac reached for the bottle, slopped more whisky into the glass, and leaned back, his head on the top of the couch, his eyes closed.

It was far too tempting. Placing her glass on the coffee table, she leaned over, pulled him against her, and wrapped her arms right around him. Zac didn't resist, instead shuffling closer to lay his head on her breast.

She was starting to get pins and needles in one leg by the time Zac moved to sit up. Broaching the subject she thought was bothering him, she said, 'Amelia's going to be a mess for a while.'

'That boy will be a mess for the rest of his life.'

'It's going to take patience and counselling, yes, but his parents will be there for him all the way. He'll make it. Hopefully he learned a huge lesson today.' Though what the kid had been thinking, taking the car for a spin in a packed garage, was beyond her.

Zac leaned forward, his elbows on his knees, the glass between his hands turning back and forth. 'You don't know what you're talking about. I do.'

Olivia leaned closer to place her hand on his thigh, her shoulder against his upper arm. 'Tell me.'

She said it so quietly that at first she didn't think he'd heard, but as she was about to repeat herself he said, 'I've been there.'

'Oh, Zac.' Her heart broke for the sadness and despair in those words.

'My brother's in a wheelchair. Because of me.'

She closed her eyes. The pain in Zac's face was too much. He hurt big-time. The load of guilt he carried must crush him at times. Tonight was one of those times. Today's event had brought back the memories in full colour. She opened her eyes and tried to eyeball him. 'Zac, I'm sorry.'

'Don't give me any platitudes, CC. I couldn't stand that.'

'You've heard them all before, huh?'

'Every last one.' He stared into his glass, the liquid golden in the light thrown by the fire. 'I prefer honesty and you've never given me anything else so please don't change tonight. No "Mark's doing fine, it's okay". No "You're forgiven so get on with your life as though it didn't happen".' The warning was issued softly, which made it all the more real.

What the heck was she supposed to say if he didn't

want to talk about it? Or did he want to say what had happened to cause his brother's injuries but couldn't get the words out? Had he changed his mind about telling her anything more? Her mind was a jumble of questions and emotions. She wanted to help him, but Zac wasn't one to ask for help. Or was that what he'd done by turning up on her doorstep?

The doorbell ringing was a welcome interruption while she tried to work out where to go with this. Grabbing the money she'd put out earlier, she went to get dinner.

Zac stood up as she returned to the sitting room. 'I'll head away and leave you in peace.'

'You're welcome to share this. I never eat more than half.' Though tonight she might've, considering the state her stomach was in. 'Sit down, Zac. I'll get some napkins and plates.'

'You want anything stronger than tea to drink?'

Was that a *Yes, I'll stay*? 'No, thanks.'

'You're cautious with your drinks, aren't you?' Zac smiled half-heartedly. 'Afraid of making an idiot of yourself?'

'Absolutely.' Rejoining him on the couch, she sighed. 'Life when I was younger was chaotic and messy. I learned to be rigid in my dealings with my mum, school, everything. Too controlled maybe, but that's how I manage.'

Taking her hand, Zac locked eyes with hers. 'Yet you're completely off the radar when it comes to sex.'

She spluttered over the mouthful she'd just bitten off her pizza.

Zac wiped her mouth with his napkin. 'I wasn't complaining.' The smile he gave her was tender, turning her inside out.

'Maybe sex is my one outlet,' she managed, holding back from explaining it hadn't been like that with the few other men she'd slept with.

He was very quiet for a few minutes, then blew her away with, 'Would you come to Fiji with me if we agreed to no sex for the whole trip?'

'What?' she asked.

'Think you—we—can do that?'

Talk about a challenge she couldn't resist. Especially as she was struggling to keep refusing to go in the first place. And now that she'd heard more about what made Zac tick she wanted to spend more time with him.

Zac grimaced. The need to go away with Olivia just got stronger and stronger, no matter how often he told himself he was making a mistake. When he'd told her about Mark he'd very nearly continued with the whole sordid story of how his life had changed for ever but a modicum of common sense had prevailed. Fear of seeing disgust in her eyes had locked his tongue to the roof of his mouth.

But if only she'd agree to go to that resort island with him. Go and have some good, honest fun. Even if she agreed to the bizarre suggestion he'd just put out there, he'd be happy. He wouldn't mind someone to talk to, to relax with.

He saw Olivia open her mouth, heard her say as though in slow motion, 'I'll go. I won't change my mind again. I'm sorry I've been vacillating.'

Excitement zipped through him, temporarily drowning out the horrors of that morning's disaster. They were going to spend time together without the pressures of work; with time to talk, to be themselves, and maybe learn more about each other. 'Good.'

'That's it?' She laughed, a tinkling sound that lightened his mood.

'Yes.' Relief softened him. 'You know what? I think it'll be great. Just the two of us.'

Olivia smiled.

It was a big, soft smile that caused him to take a risk. 'I was driving Dad's car.' Swallowing hard, he continued. 'It was late. We'd been out all day at the rugby, and stopped at a friend's on the way home.' His gut churned. 'Mark was being a pain in the arse, winding me up as only he knew how, and when we drove away from that house he said one thing too many and I lost it. Slammed my foot on the accelerator. The car spun into the stone wall along the waterfront and flipped into the water. Mark's back was broken.' That was all there was to it.

Her expression showed no condemnation. 'How awful for your family. Especially you. You've taken the blame ever since, right?'

Air huffed out of his lungs. 'Of course. I *was* at fault. I lost my temper.' *Damn, but it still hurt so badly.* If he never made another mistake in his life it wouldn't be good enough.

'You haven't forgiven yourself. Does your brother blame you?' When he nodded once, she continued. 'What about your parents? Surely they don't?'

He went for broke. 'My parents put me in charge of my brother from very early on. They were both busy with their careers as CEOs of big businesses. We were the children to be trotted out at functions or for family photos, and they were proud of us as long as we didn't stuff up. Which I did—monumentally.' At least now she'd understand why he wasn't looking for a woman to love and settle down with, that he'd always fly solo.

One holiday in Fiji being the exception. 'Of course they haven't forgiven me. I was in charge of Mark that night.'

Olivia wanted to cry for him. How could parents do that? Then again, her father had left her with Mum, hadn't he? Zac shouldn't, mustn't take all the blame, but he'd obviously made a lifelong habit of shouldering it. 'So you and Mark don't get along even now?'

'Hardly.' His mouth flattened. 'He's a successful architect, which is something to be grateful for.'

'More than something. It says he's moved on, hasn't let his spinal injury hold him back.' If only she could remove Zac's pain. But there was only one person who could do that. Zac.

'My parents pretty much disowned me after the accident.' Zac's face was bleak. 'I continued living with them for the rest of that year but it was as though I was a stranger. Come the last day of school I was gone. I got a job in a supermarket and went to live with my grandfather. Dad gave me a generous allowance but I turned him down and paid my university fees myself. I never went back home.'

And she'd thought her life had been bad. No wonder she and Zac both balked at commitment. 'That's harsh.' Actually, it was lousy. How could any parent do that? Did Zac think if he moved on, let himself stop feeling guilt, then he'd be setting himself up for another fall? Zac was a very responsible person. That had been abundantly clear when they'd been training to become surgeons. Had that come from this accident? Or had he always been a responsible person who'd made one mistake? Now she understood his outburst over the boy who'd knocked down Amelia that morning. 'I'm glad you have your grandfather.'

He cocked an eyebrow at her. 'So am I. Except he died last Christmas.' That sadness had returned to his eyes, tightened his face, more deeply, more strongly than ever.

Olivia wanted to banish it—if only for a few hours. And she only knew one way. They weren't in Fiji yet. Standing up, she put her hand out to him. 'Come with me.'

His hand was warm and firm as his fingers laced through hers. He didn't say a word as she led him down the hall to her bedroom. Or when she began unbuttoning his shirt.

Running her hands over that wide expanse of muscular chest, her blood began to thrum along her veins. Her lips surrounded his nipple, her tongue caressed slowly. Then Zac's hands were lifting her head so he could kiss her.

A long, slow kiss that had none of the urgent fire of any of their previous kisses and all the quietness of giving and sharing. It was heady stuff.

'Olivia,' Zac groaned against her mouth.

Without breaking the kiss, she pushed his shirt off his shoulders and down his arms, then found the stud and zip of his jeans. When Zac moved to lift her top she took his hands and placed them at his sides, and continued removing his jeans.

When she had him naked she gently shoved him backwards to sprawl across her bed. Her tummy quivered at the beautiful sight. His well-honed muscles accentuated his masculinity. Slowly she raised her top, exposing her bra-covered breasts. Next she slid her hands under the waistband of her shapeless trackies and began pushing them, oh, so slowly down to her hips, her thighs, her knees.

Zac's gaze followed her actions, his eyes kissing her skin. Shivers of excitement touched all the exposed places of her body. Standing in her panties and bra, she suddenly felt uncomfortable. What was she doing? Then Zac's tongue lapped his bottom lip and she relaxed. It wasn't as though he hadn't seen her naked, and while she mightn't be a strip dancer she could undress seductively.

Zac put his hands behind his head and kept watching her.

Placing one foot on the bed, she undid her bra and let it fall into her hands to be twirled across the room.

Zac's eyes widened and his tongue did another lick of his lips.

With one forefinger she began lowering her panties, never taking her eyes off his. She saw when they widened, when his chest began rising and falling faster, when his erection strained tight. Swinging a leg over his body, she hovered above him, moving so that her centre barely touched the tip of his shaft.

'Oh, sweetheart, let me touch you.' Those firm hands she craved on her skin covered her breasts, lifting them, caressing and gently squeezing them. His thumbs teased her nipples into hard, tight peaks.

Heat spread throughout her body like a slow burn, sending lazy flames of desire to every corner, warming her skin, drying her mouth. She began to lower herself over him, taking him deep inside.

Zac moved his hands to her buttocks, and he held her still. 'Not yet.'

Suddenly Olivia was on her back with Zac above her, kissing every inch of her heated skin, drowning her in need and longing. Taking his time to work down her body. They'd never made love like this.

This felt like lovemaking; not hot, frantic sex.

And when Zac moved over her, claimed her, they moved in unison, a slow rhythm that built and built till finally they reached a crescendo that stole the breath out of her lungs and sent her spinning out of control.

Olivia woke slowly. A heavy weight lay over her waist. Zac's arm. His breaths were soft on the back of her neck. His knees tucked in behind hers, and his stomach pushed against her lower back. Wow. This was amazing. Comfortable and cosy, warm and sexy. But mostly wonderful. Something she'd never experienced before. She snuggled nearer, closing her eyes to absorb every sensation moving through her. Warmth from that splayed hand on her stomach, from those thigh muscles behind her.

'Morning, beautiful,' Zac whispered against her neck.

'Wow,' she said. Hard to believe what she'd been missing out on. A small laugh escaped her. Slipping her fingers through Zac's on her stomach, she admitted, 'I've never had a man stay the night.'

Warm lips laid a soft kiss on her shoulder. 'Glad I'm the chosen one.' Another kiss. 'It's not something I normally do either.'

It was as though her whole body smiled. She and Zac had slept together, as in 'closed their eyes and gone to sleep' slept. She'd heard women talk about how good it was to sleep, spooned with their partner, and had thought they were exaggerating. Now she got it.

Careful. This was starting to feel like a relationship, as in not just about sex. Olivia tensed. Really? Damn. Just when she was beginning to enjoy things reality raised its annoying head to remind her she knew nothing about a good, solid, loving relationship between a man and a woman. Neither did Zac.

'Hey, relax. I'm not going to bite.' Zac's voice sounded sleep-laden.

No, but was he going to hurt her? Not today, or next month maybe, but eventually would he realise he didn't want to spend time with her, and walk? She had to protect herself. Wriggling free, she sat up. 'I'm going to take a shower.'

Zac reached for her, pulled her down. 'Come here. Let's stay tucked up for a little longer.'

'But…'

'Do you have to be somewhere in a hurry?' he asked reasonably.

'No.' Neither could she deny that lying in Zac's strong arms gave her a sense of belonging. Something that had been missing most of her life. Tension began tripping up her spine. Not good. Belonging went hand in hand with a serious relationship. Squeezing her eyes shut tight, she worked at banishing the negative feeling. She'd make the most of this moment; give herself something to remember later.

'I can't believe that in less than two weeks we'll be lying under palm trees.' Excitement warmed Olivia as she talked to Zac on the phone the following Thursday night. 'I'm going on holiday.'

'Says the woman who went out of her way to avoid it.' Zac's laughter rolled down the phone.

'Yeah, well, I'm glad I came to my senses. A holiday is definitely what I need. How are you getting on with sorting your surgical list?'

'Not too bad. Because Paul's taking over my private list I haven't had to change too many appointments.

Most patients I've talked to have been understanding about the change.'

Olivia grimaced. 'I wish mine were as accepting. There've been a few tears and tantrums, but I think I've got it sorted. I'll be working some long days leading up to our departure and will be busier than rush hour on the motorway.'

'Wonderful,' he groaned. 'Are you going to sleep the whole time we're away?'

'Absolutely not.' Somehow she doubted she'd sleep much at all, knowing Zac was in the same room and out of bounds. Why had he suggested that? Getting to know each other was one thing, but seriously? No sex? This would be a very interesting holiday. 'I'm going shopping for bikinis at the weekend.'

'Can I come?'

'I don't think so.' She grinned. That so wasn't happening.

'What if I waited outside the shop and took you to lunch afterwards?'

'What sort of lunch?'

'You'd have to wait and see.' Zac laughed again.

'Sorry, not happening.'

'So where do you go shopping for beach gear in the middle of winter?'

'My favourite fashion shop has an accessories section all year round. Apparently bikinis are holiday accessories. Who'd have thought it? But, then, I haven't owned a bikini in more years than I care to count.' Or gone on a holiday.

'Don't you go to the beach?' Zac asked.

'Going to the beach is a family thing, or a teen group party.' Which had been the last time she'd gone with a crowd.

'I think it's time you started getting out there and living, CC. All work and no play is not healthy.'

'Didn't you tell me how little you do outside work?' They were a right messed-up pair. 'We'll make up for it in Fiji.'

'Can't wait.' A sigh filtered down the line. 'I mean that. You have no idea how much I'm looking forward to this now that it's real.'

'Oh, but I do. After at first refusing to accept the trip, I now find I'm often daydreaming about being on the beach or swimming with the fishes. I don't remember being this excited about anything since… Well, I don't remember.'

'We are going to have a blast.' Now he was sounding like an excited schoolboy.

'Sure are.'

Another voice interrupted the moment. 'Olivia, sweetheart, where's the tonic water?' Her mother's wheedling voice grated more than usual.

'Zac, I've got to go. Talk to you again.'

'Something up? Your tone changed. Is your mother there?' He missed nothing, damn him.

'Yes, she is.' Sometimes her mother could be demanding and unrelenting in her quest for whatever today's greatest need was, and other times she'd be all sweetness and light. 'I've got to go.'

'Hey, I'm here for you.' The excitement had gone, replaced with concern. 'We can still have that lunch.'

'I'm good, Zac. Truly.'

'Olivia, tonic water. Where have you hidden it?' Mum stood in front of her, her eyes bloodshot and her tomato-red lipstick smudged on her upper lip.

'Talk to me, CC.' Zac was in her ear.

'It's complicated.' And ugly.

'Try me,' he persisted.

'Not now, Zac.' Her mother was in her face. 'Talk later. Bye.' Olivia pressed the off button, dug deep for patience. No surprise. She was all out of it. 'There's no tonic in this house.' There hadn't been any gin either until her mother had arrived with a bottle an hour ago.

'Darling, that's no way to treat your mother.'

Air hissed over Olivia's lips. 'Keeping an endless supply of gin and tonic isn't either.' She rubbed her thumbs over her eyes. 'You said there was something you wanted to talk about.'

'I think I should sell the house. It's time to move on with my life. But you're going to say no to anything I suggest.' Petulant as well.

Being one of the trustees for her mother's property and banking details came with its own set of difficulties. But if left to her own resources her mother would've gone broke long ago. 'Mum, we've discussed this so often I can't believe you'd bring the subject up again.'

'You are so unfair. About everything.'

Yep, a right old cold fish with a bank account tighter than a fish's backside. That's me. 'Where would you live if you sold? Another house? Or an apartment somewhere?'

'I could move in with you. There're more rooms here than you know what to do with.'

That was never going to happen.

Never say never.

Olivia shuddered. She did love her mother, but for sanity's sake preferred to keep her at a distance. To share the same house day in, day out would send her climbing the harbour bridge and leaping off.

CHAPTER NINE

'Tokoriki.' The helicopter pilot pointed to an island ahead of them.

Olivia gasped. 'Oh, wow, it's tiny.'

Zac grinned. 'Perfect. You won't be able to get away from me.'

She elbowed him. 'Want to spend the night outside in a hammock? Alone?'

Zac just laughed. Damn it. 'A night in a hammock would be a novelty. I wonder if there's room for two.'

She did an exaggerated eye roll. 'Not to mention mosquitoes.'

Zac stared down at the bright blue sea as the pilot brought the helicopter around to line up with the landing pad on the resort's lawn. 'Isn't it stunning?'

Olivia leaned over Zac to get a good look at the island. 'Pretty as a picture.'

'Yes.' Zac's head was right beside hers, his scent tickling her nostrils.

Pulling sideways so that she no longer touched him, she tried to ignore the buzz of excitement fizzing along her veins. Not easy in the confined space with the smell of aftershave and hot-blooded male teasing her. How was she going to remain immune to him when they'd be sharing a bure? The photos on the internet had been a reality check, like a dousing under cold water. The one large room containing an enormous bed towards the back and lounge furniture at the front looked so romantic and had set her heart racing—and that had been back at home. Couples didn't come here to sleep in separate beds. Not unless they were Zac and her.

The helicopter touched down with a bump and Olivia snapped open the clasp on her safety belt. A big, strapping Fijian man opened the door and held out his hand to help her out. Feet firmly on the ground, she looked around and was greeted by two young girls.

'*Bula,*' they said in unison, before placing leis made of pink and yellow hibiscus flowers around her and Zac's necks.

'*Bula,*' she replied.

Zac took her hand. 'Welcome to paradise.'

The bure was gorgeous, made from dark wood and covered with thatch. Wide doors and large open windows let the sea breeze through. An overhead fan spun slowly. A perfect spot for a couple to enjoy themselves and each other. Even with the sex ban? A second shower stall, outside and without a roof, made her smile. 'All the better to stargaze.'

'Come here.' Zac still held her hand and now he tugged her over the lawn to stand on the beach twenty metres from what was to be their home for five nights.

'It's going to be dark shortly,' she sighed. The day had sped by getting here.

'Let's pop the cork on that bottle of champagne I saw in an ice bucket on the coffee table. We can sit out on our front porch and pretend we do this every night after a hard day at work.'

Olivia started walking backwards so she could watch Zac. 'You're as excited as a kid on his first holiday, aren't you?' His eyes shone, his mouth the most relaxed she could ever remember it.

'I reckon. This is like my first holiday, only way better.'

'We've barely started.' She stopped so that his next step brought him right up close. Close enough to lean in and kiss that happy mouth, which she did. But when his hands spanned her waist she reluctantly pulled back. 'Sorry, I shouldn't have done that.'

'Did the rule state no kissing?' He was shaking his head at her, his smile only increasing. Was nothing going to mar his enjoyment? 'I must've missed that.'

'Maybe you didn't put it in.' She hoped not. Kissing Zac was too much fun not to be able to do it whenever she wanted. But then there'd be consequences. Looking around for something else to talk about, she spied two hammocks slung between nearby trees. 'There's your bed. You even get a choice.'

'I am not spending my nights slapping at the mozzies, thank you very much.' Zac caught her hand, laced his fingers through hers, then swung their joined hands up to his lips and kissed her knuckles.

Careful. That might start a fire I can't put out. And we have rules. She slipped her hand out of Zac's. 'Where's that champagne?'

He tried not to look disappointed, but she saw it and felt a heel. He'd only been having fun, and she *had* instigated the kiss.

Inside, Zac picked up the card leaning against the bucket in which the ice was rapidly turning to liquid. 'Compliments of Andy and Kitty. They say thanks for the gala night and hope we have a wonderful time.'

'That's lovely. It's not as though they haven't got enough to think about at the moment.'

Minutes later they sat in front of their bure and watched the sun turning the sky red and yellow. 'That's an abrupt change from day to night,' Zac commented.

'Guess that's the tropics for you. Hard to believe we left winter behind.' The warm, heavy air made her clothes stick to her skin. She wouldn't be wearing much for the next few days.

'What's your favourite season?' Zac asked.

'Summer, followed by summer. I hate being cold.'

'Yet you bought an old villa that must be freezing in winter. Though, come to think of it, I didn't notice a chill when I was there.'

'First thing I did was improve the insulation in the roof and some of the walls. Then I had that firebox installed to replace the open fire. There's also a heat pump in the hall.'

Zac chuckled. 'I bought a very modern apartment and you went for the opposite.'

'I love old villas. There's something magical about them. Yes, they come with loads of problems, but get them sorted and there's an amazing home waiting to be loved.' She sipped her champagne. 'There's history in the boards. When I bought the place the vendors passed on to me a book written about the family who originally built it. The man had been an excise officer and his wife a nurse in the First World War.'

'So you're a history buff.'

'Only when it comes to my property, but it's neat knowing about the original owners.' She laughed softly. 'It was also a surprise finding I enjoy working on the redecorating. In spring I'm going to start putting in a garden to grow a few salad vegetables.'

'I saw your pot plants in your hallway. Just go to the markets. That way you won't starve.'

'Thanks, pal.' He was right. She always forgot to water the plants until they were drooping over the edges of their pots.

'You grew up in Auckland, right?'

She nodded. 'Remuera.' One of Auckland's most sought-after areas, where many of the city's wealthy lived. On a street where fences were metres high, hiding a multitude of sins. 'I went to a private school for girls, played the cello and joined the debating team.' That was after the in-crowd had worked their number on her because her mother had followed her around dressed in identical outfits to hers, trying to look way younger than she was.

'Was your childhood home another old house?'

She blinked, got back on track. Her mother wasn't welcome on this holiday. 'Yes. A massive, six-bedroom edifice with half an acre of gardens, a tennis court and a swimming pool.'

'You played tennis?' He didn't hide his astonishment.

'Me run around chasing a ball to bang it back over a net? Not likely.'

They were getting close to things she didn't want to talk about when she was sitting in paradise. 'I can't wait to go snorkelling amongst the fishes.'

Zac went with her change as easily as butter melted on warm toast. 'We should take a boat trip to Treasure Island and the marine reserve where the best array of fish is supposed to be.'

Zac had done some research before they'd left Auckland. She hadn't had the time. 'Five days might not be enough.'

How was he going to cope with not getting up close and naked? Zac grimaced. This magical setting was working mischief on his libido. What had he been thinking when he'd come up with that brainwave? Hadn't been thinking, that was the trouble. Now his body was screaming out for Olivia's, and he had no one to blame but himself.

'Want a top-up?' was the only lame excuse he could come up with in a hurry for getting out of the cane chair and putting some air between them for a moment.

'Of course.' When she handed him her glass she seemed to take desperate measures to prevent her fingers touching his.

Phew. Damn. Hell. He dragged his hand down over his hair. Less than an hour and he was a cot case. Certifiable. Had he been so desperate to come here with Olivia he'd have bargained with the devil if it had meant she'd agree? Seems like it. Didn't make any sense, though.

Back on the porch he passed over a full glass. 'Drink up. That ice bucket is now a water receptacle and the fridge is warmer than my toaster on full.'

'Do we get dinner brought over? I'm kind of relaxed and comfortable now.'

And I'm in need of space and people around to break the grip you have on me. I am so not ready to spend all evening alone with you when I can't touch you. 'I'm thinking dining on the restaurant deck with candles under those palm trees would be special.'

'I guess you're right.' When Olivia yawned there was nothing ladylike about her.

He grinned. 'That's it? No argument?' Then she must be very tired.

'If I stay here I'll be asleep by seven, and probably awake again by midnight.' Her throat worked as she swallowed.

'CC? You all right?'

Olivia stood up and took a step to the edge of the porch. 'Yeah,' she huffed out over the lawn. 'Good and dandy.' Her voice sounded anything but.

Moving quietly, Zac stepped up beside her, rubbed his shoulder lightly against hers. Gave her a moment to regroup her thoughts. But *his* brain wasn't quiet as it tossed up questions about this sudden mood swing. Was Olivia regretting the trip already? His stomach plummeted. Please, not that. No matter what happened after they left the island, he wanted this time with Olivia. Wanted them to have fun and be relaxed, to enjoy each other's company. He felt rather than heard her soft sigh. A gentle lifting of her shoulder against his.

'I'm afraid.'

Or that's what he thought she'd whispered. Olivia afraid? Of what? Him? The urge rose to rant at her, to tell her he'd never hurt her. But reason caught him in time. If she'd ever believed he'd hurt her she wouldn't have come near him, certainly wouldn't be on this island with him. 'Want to talk about it?'

'No.' She spoke to the dark space in front of them. Then after a minute, in a stronger tone, 'Let's go eat.' Back in control of her emotions.

Which bugged the hell out of Zac. How was he supposed to get behind the walls she put up when she kept doing this? He wanted to shake her, shake out her story, then begin to help her move past whatever locked her up so tight. But one look at that jutting chin said that now wasn't the moment. Though when would be the right time was a mystery to him. Olivia had made self-control an art form.

The only place he'd seen her enjoy herself completely, without thought for anything else, was in the sack. Light-bulb moment. Because when she'd finished she could, and did, put on her corporate-style clothes again and the control they represented.

For which he should be glad, but wasn't.

A vision of Olivia in track pants and a sweatshirt. That night she'd started making love to him and it had been as different from any other time as north was to south. Slow and tender, giving and sharing.

For him it had been a game changer. Waking up in her bed in the morning had been a first. Lying tucked up against her back, his arm over her waist, holding her close, had been another first, and absolutely wonderful, like nothing he'd experienced before. So wonderful he'd settle for cuddling Olivia all night to wake up like that again.

Okay, he'd try, but it wouldn't be easy. But he'd try really hard. *Hard is the wrong word, buddy.*

'You plan on daydreaming all night?' the woman causing these thoughts called from the door.

'Why is it called daydreaming when I'm doing it at night?'

As they strolled along the lantern-lit path Zac found himself wondering for the first time ever if he was wrong to stick to his guns and deliberately deny himself a future that involved a beautiful, loving woman and maybe equally beautiful and loving children.

No, he couldn't be wrong. How else did he justify keeping Olivia at arm's length?

Later, Olivia slid beneath the bedcovers and tucked the sheet under her neck like a prissy girl from the convent.

Zac laughed. Long and loud. His eyes twinkled and his gorgeous mouth looked good enough to devour.

'It's not that funny.' She tried not to laugh too, and only succeeded in making hysterical squawking noises instead.

'Yeah, it is, when you think what we've got up to in beds before.'

That dampened down her mirth. 'You want to change the rules.'

'Damn right I do. I'd be lying if I said otherwise.' He came and sat on the edge of the bed, on his side; no sign of laughter in his face now. 'But I'm enjoying our time together. It's like nothing we've ever done before and it's...' He waved his hand in the air between them. 'Does fun sound boring?'

'Fun is good.'

'I want to get to learn more about you, what makes you tick, the things that you'd choose to do first if time was running out. Hell, I want to know everything about you. Before the gala night I didn't know anything about you despite having spent many hours in your company.'

Wow. Really? Of course, he didn't know what he was asking for. 'We trained together. You can't do that without learning some things.' But she was ducking for cover, and that wasn't fair. 'Doctor things, I guess. Like how much you care about your patients, how intelligent you are, oh, and how pig-headed you can be.'

'Thanks a bunch.' Zac smiled. 'Okay, random question. Do you still play the cello?' He leaned back against the headboard and stretched his legs all the way down the bed.

She laughed. 'No way. I sold my cello to buy an amazing pair of leather boots that were the envy of every girl at school.' Which was why she'd wanted them. Now she bought the most amazing pairs of boots any time because she could, and loved them without needing any acknowledgement from others.

'I bet you were good at music.'

'Try very average on a good day. I think the music teacher only persisted with my lessons because he needed a cello in the school orchestra and no one else wanted to be hauling such a large instrument on and off the bus.'

'Why are you doing that?'

'What?'

'Putting yourself down again. You're a highly skilled surgeon, yet right now you're sounding like you don't believe in yourself.'

'I'm not perfect, can't excel at everything I do. For example, the pot plants in my house. But I am honest.' Most of the time.

Zac reached for her hand and held it between both of his. 'I know.'

Warm fuzzies uncurled inside her. It would be all too easy to lean her head against his chest and pretend they were a couple, a real couple with a history and a future that involved more than bedroom antics. The couple that woke up in the morning in each other's arms.

Pulling her hand free, she shuffled further down the bed. 'Time to get some sleep. Sunrise is early around these parts.' As if she'd fall asleep with Zac barely inches away from her. Those pillows she'd stuffed down the middle as a barrier were a joke, and would take two seconds to get shot of. She could only hope his mental barrier was stronger. Hers was weakening.

'Good night, Olivia.' Zac leaned over and dropped the softest, sweetest kiss of her life on her forehead. 'I'll sit out on the porch for a while.'

If he was cross at her abrupt withdrawal he wasn't

showing it. But, then, he was good at hiding his feelings behind a smile or laughter. This time the smile was stretched a little too tight, and his eyes held a tinge of sadness.

'Zac,' she called as he reached the door leading outside. 'Thanks.'

His eyebrow rose in query. 'For?'

'Being you, caring and understanding.'

Understanding? Zac growled under his breath. *Newsflash, CC, I don't understand a thing. Whatever's going on between us is a complete mystery. What I want is no longer clear. I feel like I'm walking in deep mud and every now and then stepping onto a dry patch. A brief moment of hope before sliding back into the mire.*

His right foot pushed against the ground to set the hammock swinging. Stretched full length, he linked his hands together behind his head. The dark sky twinkled with so many stars it was as though a kid had lit up a whole pack of sparklers. The hammock was unbelievably comfortable. So far the mosquitoes hadn't found him. Hopefully when they did, he'd put enough insect repellent on what little skin was exposed to deter them.

His heart was back in the bure, lying next to Olivia. His mind was seeing the despair and fear that sometimes altered her expression and briefly filled those eyes that usually reminded him of flowers. Whatever had caused her grief, she wasn't prepared to talk about it. Yet.

Come on. Why should she choose to bare her soul to him?

Because they were connected. They mightn't have known it before but the threads were becoming more obvious by the day. They both had issues holding them back from getting into a serious relationship. What Olivia's troubles were he had no idea, but they were there. He recognised his own stock standard coping mechanisms in her now that he'd started looking for them.

He wanted to hold her, protect her for ever.

Kind of strange for a guy who had no plans to commit to settling down. Yet all the reasons for why he shouldn't were slipping away, one by one dropping off the edge, leaving him exposed and cautious yet strangely ready to try for the rainbow.

Was Olivia the pot of gold at the end of his rainbow?

No. There wasn't any rainbow. The hardest lesson of his life had been that night of the accident when he'd learned his parents didn't love him unconditionally. Didn't love him enough to support and help him through the trauma of what he'd done. Sometimes he wondered if they'd loved him and Mark at all; as in deep, for ever, parent kind of love. Their careers had been their priority, taking all their time and concentration, with nothing left over for their sons. *Why did they have children?* They clearly hadn't wanted to be with their sons. Zac had asked his grandfather about it on numerous occasions but Grampy hadn't been able to come up with a satisfactory answer. Not one he was prepared to tell his grandson anyway.

Zac swallowed the usual bile that came from thinking about his parents. Coming from a dysfunctional family, the odds were he'd be bad at parenting too. Another reason not to settle down with a wonderful woman and contemplate the picket-fence scenario.

Zac's sigh was long and slow. Around him everything had gone quiet, and lights were being turned off. With nothing to do after dinner most people would be settled in their bures. He pushed with his foot again, swinging the hammock high, sighing as the movement slowed and the arc became less and less. Beyond the edge of the lawn the waves rolled up the sand, then pulled away, rolled in, pulled away.

'Zac, come inside.'

Someone was shaking his arm gently.

'Come on. Wake up. You're getting wet from the dew.'

Hauling his eyelids up, he saw her leaning over him, her long hair framing her face. 'Olivia.' His Olivia.

'The one and only.' She tugged at him. 'You can't spend the whole night out here.'

Swinging his legs over the side, he awkwardly pushed out of the hammock. 'What time is it?'

'One o'clock.' She took his hand and led him inside to that damned bed with its row of pillows down the middle.

Zac shucked out of his shirt and trousers, jerked the bedcover back and threw the pillows on the floor. Dropping into bed, he reached for Olivia where she now lay on her side, facing him. 'Roll over,' he whispered. 'I want to hold you all night.'

If only it were that easy.

CHAPTER TEN

AT THE END of the next day Zac stretched his legs out and laced his fingers behind his head. He would not think about night number two and lying beside Olivia again. Nope, he'd have a drink and watch the sunset. 'Come on, woman, bring me that beer you promised.'

'Sack the last slave, did you?'

'Hell, no. She's good for bed gymnastics.' So much for not thinking about bed.

'For that you're going to have to wait. Or, novel idea, get your own drink.' Olivia laughed. 'I'm changing out of my bikini.'

Phew. Those two narrow strips of red fabric had kept his head in a spin all day. Had had him swimming in the sea four times, and in the pool once. Then there'd been the cold shower half an hour ago. He'd even taken a kayak out to paddle around the island. Anything to keep busy and the need strumming through his veins under control. Huh. As if. One look at Olivia and his blood was boiling and his crotch tightening. This sex ban would be his undoing. Who knew what state he'd be in by the time he got back to Auckland? Ruined for ever, probably.

'Here.'

An icy bottle appeared before his eyes. 'Thank you,

and whoever's responsible for these things.' Then he made the mistake of looking at Olivia and pressed the bottom of the bottle over his manhood. The bikini would've been preferable.

'You're staring.' She sank onto the deckchair beside him. 'You don't like my dress?'

While the skimpy piece of floral material did cover more of that exquisite body than the bikini had, the way the fabric draped was plain punishing. Mouth-watering, muscle-tightening, hormone-fizzing, blood-heating cruel. 'You call that a dress?' he hissed over dry lips.

She laughed, low and sexy. 'Well, it's not a T-shirt.'

How in hell was he to sit here drinking beer and not choke? Then he had to take her to dinner where every male on the island was going to gag, and their women would beat them around the head. 'You're a danger to mankind.'

'I'll change before dinner. Put a T-shirt on.'

'Does that come with trousers?' The beer was cold in his over-hot mouth; cool as it slid past the lump in his throat. One bottle wasn't enough. Holding out his empty one, he growled in a mock bossy tone, 'Another one, as soon as possible.' His eyes were fixed on the horizon, glazed over for all he could see. His imagination was so busy dealing with pictures of Olivia's hot bod and that handkerchief that was apparently a dress, nothing else about him seemed to be in good working order. Except the one muscle he wasn't allowed to use.

'Here you go, sir.' A bottle held around the neck by slim fingers waved in front of his face.

He was going insane. Had to be. Grabbing the bottle, he raised it to his lips and gulped. *Do something. Talk about anything, just get your brain working.* Glancing around, he came up with, 'So you're not into spiders.'

Olivia shuddered. 'Not at all, but until today I thought one the size of my thumbnail was a problem. But those things hanging over the path in webs wider than our bed?' Another shudder. 'Ugh. You were my hero, clearing those monsters out of the way.'

Our bed? This wasn't helping. He tried again. 'The outlook from the top of the hill showed how small the island is.' Not exactly scintillating conversation. 'It's hard to imagine living on such a tiny spot in the ocean. I'd go stir-crazy if this was home for me.'

'I guess if you're born here it's what you're used to.'

'Have you ever thought how lucky we are just because of where we were born?' Deep, Zac, boy. And diverting. 'Imagine how different our lives would be if we'd been born in the Sahara, or on the Indian continent.'

'I'd have five kids and look ready to retire, except that wouldn't be an option.' Olivia grinned. 'You're right. It does come down to luck.'

'I'm going to give that fishing a crack tomorrow. Donny—he's the gardener—is lending me a hand line.'

The guy had strolled up to him as he'd watched the local men work the sudden rush of fish churning up the water at the shoreline and told him, 'Trevally chase the Pacific sardines into the beach in a feeding frenzy. It happens about twice a day at this time of year.'

'Do the men catch many?' Zac had asked.

'Good days and bad days. No one relies on trevallies as a regular supply of food for the family.'

'I've never seen anyone use a hand line and no rod. The skin on those men's hands must be tough.' Zac had introduced himself and before he'd known it he'd had a fishing date for tomorrow. 'I haven't fished since I was a kid and Grampy took me out.'

Olivia was chuckling. 'This I have to see. The immaculate surgeon getting his hands stinky from fish.'

'I'm taking that as a positive sign. You obviously think I'll catch one.'

'And if you do? What will you do with it?'

He hadn't thought that far ahead. 'Ask the chef to cook it for us? Other people must've caught fish and taken them to the kitchen.'

'Talking of kitchens, shall we stroll across to the outdoor lounge for a cocktail before dinner? I've never had one but this seems the place to give it a try.'

'Good idea.' Hopefully there'd be some diversions from that dress. 'You'll get one of those tacky little umbrellas to keep as a souvenir.' He grinned.

'Thought I'd start with a mimosa.' She returned his grin.

'Start? Are we in for a session?'

She shook her head, that shiny mane sliding over her shoulders. 'You want me off my face and losing my mind?'

If it meant forgetting their promise—then, yes. But if he was being a gentleman—then, no.

'I've caught one,' Zac shouted triumphantly early the next morning as he wound the hand line in as fast as possible.

'What? A sardine?' Olivia teased. She'd strolled down the beach to join him, after opting for a leisurely start to the day by reading in bed after Donny had knocked on the door to tell Zac the fish were running.

'A damned big trevally,' Zac scowled. 'This nylon's hard on the hands.'

'Toughen up. You don't see the locals complaining.' Looking along the beach, she could see two Fijian men also winding in taut lines. 'You've got to get in the water and use your foot to scoop the fish up onto the sand.'

'Glad I've got an expert telling me what to do.' He started walking backwards up the beach, hauling his catch out of the water. 'Look at that beauty.'

Trying not to laugh, she bent down to admire Zac's fish. 'Should keep a toddler from starving.'

'Any time you want to go read your book again feel free. This is man stuff. Where's Donny?'

'Donny,' Olivia called to the man standing further up the beach. 'Zac's caught something.'

As he wandered close Donny nodded. 'Not bad for a first time.'

'I guess that means I'm going to release it back into the water.' Zac sighed, and carefully removed the hook.

'Wait, photo opportunity.' Olivia snapped a quick shot as Zac ignored the camera.

'Wait till I get a proper fish.' He held the fish in the water until it swam away, then threw the line as far beyond the churning water as possible so he could draw the hook through the seething trevally.

Olivia sat down, her elbows on her knees, and watched him. Never had she seen him so relaxed. He was concentrating so much he didn't notice her snap a couple more photos. This holiday was showing her a different Zac. She particularly liked the one who'd tossed those pillows aside to hold her against him while they'd tried to go to sleep.

The climate had done a line on them, spoiling that hug, though probably saving her from having to haul the brakes on the raw need that had begun filling her. The humidity had made her skin slick and her body uncomfortably hot in a way that had had nothing to do with sex. They'd rolled apart after twenty minutes. Unbelievably, she'd fallen into a deep sleep not long after. Had to be because she'd felt so secure with this Zac who could take a night off the passion. She'd never spent a night just sleeping with a man. That spoke of intimacies too close for comfort, yet now she craved it with Zac more than anything.

A shudder ripped through her, disturbing in its intensity. Was she seriously in danger of falling for him? Unlikely. She only had to think of her parents' marriage to knock those ideas into place.

Zac tossed a fist in the air. 'Got another one.'

Olivia jumped up and went to stand beside him, eager to enjoy the moment and drop the past for a while. If only it was that easy to dump for ever.

Zac was focused intently on getting his catch on shore. 'Want fish for breakfast?'

'Breakfast of any kind would be good.'

Zac wound furiously. 'This one's definitely bigger than the last baby.'

'That's a good trevally,' Donny agreed minutes later.

'Will the chef cook it for me?' Zac asked.

'Yes, or my wife could use it to make you a traditional Fijian meal to have at our house tonight.'

'Really? Your family would join us?' When Donny nodded, he continued, 'That would be fantastic.'

Olivia asked, 'What do we bring?'

'Nothing. We eat at five thirty because our grandson goes to bed early.'

'You have a grandchild living with you? Bet you love that.'

'His mother's our daughter. She does the massages in the spa.'

Olivia smiled. 'Then I'll meet her this afternoon. I'm booked in for a full body massage at two o'clock.'

Zac laughed. 'Think she'll be better than me?'

She looked away to hide the sudden flush creeping up her cheeks. 'No comment.'

Donny and his wife, Lauan, greeted Olivia and Zac warmly, welcoming them into the small thatch bungalow crowded with relatives. It felt as if half the island's population was there. The fish hadn't been that big, Olivia thought as she sat down on the woven flax mat in front of a larger one with plates stacked at one end.

Zac was soon chatting with the men and Olivia tried to look around without appearing nosey. Apart from her, all the other females were seated behind the circle enclosing that mat. 'Lauan,' she said quietly. 'I can sit with you.'

Lauan shook her head. 'You're a visitor.'

Yes, but I'd love to be with the women. Unfortunately it would be rude to protest. 'I've been looking forward to coming here all day. How do you cook the fish?'

'I wrap it in banana leaves to steam over the open fire. There is coconut milk added, and potatoes. Thank your husband for the fish.'

Husband? To the locals they probably did appear to be a married couple. 'I will.'

Lauan squatted beside her. 'I've also made a chicken stew with carrots, potatoes, and broccoli.' She rolled her eyes softly. 'Too many people for one fish. But they all wanted to meet you.'

Thinking of the scrawny chickens she'd seen pecking around the base of the trees behind the resort, Olivia wondered if one chook would go any further than the fish. All part of the adventure. 'I'm happy to meet you all.' She nodded to the women.

Two of them disappeared into another room and

soon large plates of steaming food were being placed on the mat.

'That smells delicious,' Olivia said.

'Doesn't it,' Zac agreed. Leaning closer, he asked, 'You okay?'

'Absolutely. I'm glad you caught that sucker, or we might never have had this opportunity.' She took the plate of food handed to her and looked for cutlery, feeling silly when there wasn't any. When in Fiji do as the Fijians do. But as she placed a piece of fish in her mouth a fork appeared in front of her.

'For you.'

Zac got one too. 'Thanks, but I'll use my fingers.'

The food was simple and tasty, the vegetables so fresh they must've been picked only hours ago. 'Sometimes I think we forget the pleasure of plain food.' Olivia noticed a child peeking around at her from behind Donny.

'Hello. What's your name?'

The child ducked back.

Remembering Donny's earlier conversation on the beach, she asked Lauan, 'Your grandson?'

'Yes. Josaia. He's shy.'

'I hope he comes over to say hello while we're here.'

'After dinner.'

But it seemed Josaia couldn't wait to take another peek, and Olivia winked at him.

When he winked back she felt she'd won a prize. Her mouth widened into a smile and she was rewarded with one in return. When dinner was finished she did get to see the boy properly when he came close to pick up the empty plates at his grandmother's bidding. Olivia's heart rolled. One of his arms was stiff and awkward, and his left cheek marred by terrible scarring.

Josaia knew she'd seen and his smile vanished as he twisted his head away from her. When he reached out for her plate she picked it up and placed it in his hand. 'Thank you,' she said. 'Where do you go to school?'

Donny was watching her guardedly. 'The kids go to the mainland for school.'

That didn't answer her specific question but she knew when to mind her own business.

Josaia disappeared with his load of plates, and she suspected she wouldn't be seeing him again tonight.

Donny tugged his shoulders back. 'He doesn't go to school because other children tease him. I try to teach him, but he's missing out on so much.'

What had happened to cause that disfiguring scar? She felt sure he hadn't seen a plastic surgeon. That wound had been too crudely sutured. Maybe she could help in some way. But was it her place to ask? It might be better coming from Zac. Man-to-man stuff. Leaning sideways, she gave him a wee nudge and got the slightest of nods.

He asked, 'Did Josaia have an accident here on the island?'

The older man nodded, his eyes so sad Olivia felt her heart slow. *He's broken-hearted for his grandson.* 'Last year Josaia was swimming with a group of his mates when a tourist joined them, asking about the fish and where he should go to try out his spear gun.'

Zac asked softly, 'Josaia was shot with a spear gun?'

Olivia stifled a gasp. *Josaia is lucky to be alive.* She slipped her hand between Zac's arm and his side, wrapped her fingers around his elbow.

Zac continued in the same low, calm voice. 'Where was Josaia treated?'

'On the mainland. In the hospital. It's a good hospital, but no one knew what to do for my grandson. I begged the doctors send him to Australia or New Zealand. They said it wasn't possible, and Josaia would be all right once they stitched him up and set his broken bones.' Tears streamed down the proud man's face. 'I begged them to rethink. He's only seven.'

'There's nothing wrong with him.' Lauan's voice was sharp and angry. 'But you'd think he was a leper from the way boys who used to be his friends laugh at him now.'

'That's so hard for anyone, but especially a child.'

'He was always so popular until the accident.' Donny stared at a spot on the dining mat. 'His mother works hard to raise money to take him away for help. His father works in Australia to make money.'

'When was the last time Josaia saw his dad?' Olivia asked, her heart thudding.

'Christmas.'

Seven months ago. What sort of life was that for a young boy? Not to have his dad there had to be hard. Olivia knew about that. She wanted to slap the floor and say she'd see that Josaia got whatever he needed and as soon as possible, but despite the urgent need to help this boy she held her tongue. She'd talk this through with Zac first.

Zac knew Olivia was barely holding herself together for the remainder of their time with Donny's family. He could see the sadness in her face, feel the need for her to do something to rectify what had happened with Josaia. But most of all he understood how much she was struggling to hold it all in so that she didn't make rash promises she mightn't be able keep and thereby hurt the family further.

The meal was over early by their standards. As they walked away from their hosts Zac draped an arm over Olivia's shoulders. 'I'd like a drink.'

'I could go a cup of tea.'

'We can discuss what you're desperate to do for Josaia.'

'That poor kid. I bet the worst part of the whole deal is the way his old friends are now treating him. Children are cruel.' She shuddered.

'Insecurities, jealousy, wanting to be popular with the in-crowd. Anything and everything. Even plain old nastiness.' The sudden tension in her fingers suggested she'd had her share of being on the outside. But of course. She'd said she'd worked hard to be liked and be a part of the group at med school. 'This is why you want to help Josaia? Apart from the medical point of view?'

They'd reached the outdoor lounge at the main building by the time she answered. 'That boy is surrounded by people who love him, but they're all adults. There don't appear to be any children in his life. At first I thought that was because it was the end of the day and everyone would be at home, except when we walked to Donny's house there were kids playing behind the huts.'

'Then we saw his face and heard the despair in his grandparents' voices.'

'You're onto it.'

Zac pulled out a chair for Olivia at an outside table. 'What are you having?'

A wicked twinkle lit up her eyes, banishing that sadness for a boy she'd barely met. 'You know what? Forget tea. Make that a cocktail.' She looked around. 'Where's a menu?'

'What about PS I…' His voice trailed off at the realisation of what he'd been about to say. It was only the name of a drink, but the import of the words he hadn't finished were slowly sinking in, one by one, adding up to a frightening whole.

'Zac? What's up? Are you all right?'

The concern in her tone wound around him, added to his confusion. Had he really been going to say 'PS I love you'? Shaking his head, he sank onto a chair, putting a gap between them. But her eyes followed, as did that floral scent she wore. Or was that the smell of the frangipani growing a metre away?

'Zac.' Her eyes widened. 'You're worrying me.'

'I'm fine.' *Really? This palpitating heart thing is fine? The knot in your gut is A-okay? The sweat on your palms due to the humidity?* 'Sorry. There's a cocktail made with amaretto, Kahlúa, and Irish cream that's perfect for after dinner. Very creamy and sweet, like a dessert, which you've missed out on tonight.' Blah, blah, blah. Shoving up onto his feet, he asked, 'Will that do?' Ordering drinks would give him the space he needed right now.

'Sounds good.' Olivia nodded, looking perplexed. As well she should. Did she know she was with a lunatic?

Moving through the tables full of happy diners, Zac tried to ignore the questions battering his brain. He'd been enjoying getting to know Olivia better, happy being with her, wanted more time together. So why the hell hadn't he ever considered he might be falling for her?

Because love spelt commitment. *Commitment isn't the problem.* No. It wasn't. *It's the responsibility.* That went with any relationship, whether the other person was his best friend, his lover, or his brother. He loved Mark, had done from the day his tiny, wriggly body had been placed in his arms. Yet he'd still managed to screw up in a very big way, changing Mark's life for ever.

'Yes, sir. What would you like?'

Zac shook his head and stared across the bar at the woman waiting patiently for him to tell her what drinks he wanted. 'A whisky on the rocks. Make it a double. And do you know a cocktail called PS I Love You?'

She frowned. 'Not sure, but we've got a book describing most cocktails.'

When Zac told her the ingredients she smiled. 'We call it Love on the Wind. I'll bring the drinks across to you.'

He wasn't ready to return to Olivia. 'I'll have that whisky now.' And ordered a second to take with him.

Olivia watched him placing her glass on the table, returning to his seat. He waited for her to ask why he'd taken so long, and was grateful when she didn't.

'Where do we start with Josaia's case? Talk to his family, or go to the mainland to check out the hospital and see if I can do a surgery there?'

'Why not take him back to Auckland for the operation? If there's going to be one. You've only seen that horrendous scar from across the room in dim light. There might be nothing you can do.'

She sipped her Love on the Wind—he would not think of it as PS I Love You—and smiled. Her tongue did a lap of her lips. 'That's amazing.'

So was the way his heart squeezed and his insides softened. Of course his libido sat up to attention. That was a given around this woman. What was extraordinary was that she didn't know about this new effect she was having on him. He'd have sworn there were signs written all over his face. 'Glad you like it. About Josaia and what to do first.' He had to talk, about anything except them, and talk lots.

Olivia said, 'Operating back home might be preferable so we get the best people on side for Josaia. It's going to involve huge expense for the family, though. Hospital costs, accommodation, flights, and other incidentals I can't think of right now.'

'I doubt there's a lot of spare money in that household.' He locked his eyes on hers. 'You're going to throw in your time for free.'

'Of course.'

'I want to look at that shoulder. There might be something I can do there.' See, he could move on from those other thoughts that had swamped his brain. 'First we'll talk to Donny. If he's willing to take this further, we'll decide how to go about it.'

Olivia's hand covered his, and her fingers curled around his. 'We have a plan.'

'You like plans, don't you?'

'They keep me centred.'

So what was her plan for the rest of the night? It wouldn't be what he hoped for. She'd be keeping to the other plan. Zac drained his glass, trying not to bemoan the fact he'd set the rule in the first place.

CHAPTER ELEVEN

THE ARRAY OF fish in every colour imaginable stole Olivia's breath away when she sank beneath the sea's surface off Treasure Island. She automatically reached out for Zac's hand and tugged him down beside her. 'Unbelievable,' she spluttered in her mouthpiece, even though he couldn't hear her.

When Zac looked her way she saw the same amazement in his face. When he started stroking through the water, heading further out from the shore, she followed. She'd never seen anything like this. When Zac paused she swam up beside him to lean in against his body. Skin to skin underwater. Delicious and exciting. And then there were the fish. One big, fat, enjoyable picture.

Olivia kicked her flippers slowly so as not to disturb the dainty creatures too much and followed a group of yellow and blue fish. Then a larger orange one swam through the middle, scattering the others. Yellow and blue fish. Orange fish. She grinned. Very technicolour. Down here it was like a moving painting: sharp colours, delicate manoeuvres, majestic shapes—and innocence. As though these creatures had no enemies. Which was probably far from the truth, though at least they were safe from mankind. This was a sanctuary, and the results were stunning. The numbers and varieties of fish were unbelievable.

'That's magic down there.' Zac echoed her thoughts when they finally crawled out of the water and flopped onto the sand.

'I've been missing out on so much by not travelling.' She lay on her back, arms and legs spread in the sun. 'It's one of those things on my to-do-one-day list. Think it's time to make that a do-it-now list.'

'Shame your mother hated flying.'

'Didn't matter.' Olivia sat up and started brushing off the sand, which was scratchy on her skin. 'Dad left when I was twelve.'

'That's tough.'

She swallowed hard. 'Mum was—is—an alcoholic.' Swallow. She couldn't look at Zac. 'As in often totally crazy, uncontrollable, off-the-rails alcoholic. Dad ran out of patience.'

'How the hell did you cope?' Zac's hand covered hers.

'Not sure I did, really.' Spill the rest. 'I tried becoming a part of the school in-crowd so that I could forget what went on at home. Failed big-time because of Mum. Everyone knew what she was.'

'Where did the cello fit in?' Zac was giving her breathing space.

'When I didn't make it as an in-person I went for the nerd brigade.' She huffed out a tight laugh. 'That probably saved me, considering where some of the girls I'd desperately wanted to befriend ended up while I was at med school.'

'Why medicine?'

She shrugged. 'No idea. It was just something I

wanted to do. As a little girl my dolls were always covered in plasters and bandages.'

'At least you'd have been sure of your choice, then.'

'You weren't?'

Zac grimaced. 'I started university intending to become an engineer.'

'What changed your mind?'

'Seeing my brother going through rehab and getting no end of help from doctors along the way made me think I'd be happier doing medicine.'

'Your parents didn't sway you?'

'Put it this way, Dad's an engineer at the top of his game, being the CEO for one of the country's largest steelworks.'

'You wanted to follow him into the business?'

'No, I wanted to gain acknowledgement that I was his son.'

Reaching for his hand, Olivia said, 'That's the wrong reason to choose a career.'

'I was desperate.'

She shuddered. 'I understand.' Seemed she wasn't the only one with difficult parents. 'Being an only child, I was never really treated as a kid even before Dad left.' Not wanting to spoil a wonderful day with talk of her childhood, she said, 'Let's go eat lunch by the pool. All that fish-gazing has made me hungry.'

Zac scrambled to his feet and held out his hand, hauling her upright with one easy, fluid movement. 'I could murder a beer. Think I've swallowed a litre of salt water.'

'Yuk.' Around at the front of the resort Olivia dived into the pool, eager to get rid of the salt and sand on her skin. When she hauled herself up over the side Zac was sitting at a nearby table, beer in hand, and his gaze fixed on her. Suddenly her bikini felt non-existent. A pool attendant handed her a towel and she quickly dried off before pulling on a sleeveless shirt and shorts and joining Zac under the coconut palms. 'Food and water, I think.'

Zac pushed a bottle and glass towards her. 'Sparkling water, as requested.'

Turning her hand over, she slipped her fingers between his and enjoyed the moment. This was something she hadn't known before. She had never spent time just holding a man's hand without sex being the ultimate goal. Unbelievable how wonderful it felt. Full of promise without any expectations.

A group of children was leaping into the deep end of the pool, splashing half the contents over the side while shrieking their heads off.

'They're fun but I'm glad glad we're not staying here on Treasure Island when Tokoriki is a no-go zone for kids,' Zac commented. 'I don't mean anything nasty by that, but as a childless adult I don't really want to share my rare break with other people's offspring.'

'I get it.' She took a risk. 'You think you'll ever have children? Once you find a life partner, I mean.'

Zac's eyes widened, and his mouth alternated between a smile and a grimace. 'Now, there's a loaded question. Or two.'

'It wasn't meant as such.' *Wasn't it?* 'Just wondering if you were planning on having a family and a house in the burbs.' Geez, what would she answer if he turned the question back at her?

The level in his beer glass dropped as he drank and stared at the kids in the pool. 'You know what? I'd love to have children of my own.' The surprise in his voice told her plenty.

'Isn't that a natural thing for most people to want?'

'Yeah, but after Mark's accident I decided I wasn't having a family. Too easy to hurt them.' Again he raised his glass to his lips and sipped the beer thoughtfully. 'I think I've been wrong. I do want children.' His head jerked backwards as though he couldn't quite get his mind around this revelation.

Little Zacs. Olivia let the breath that had stalled in her lungs dribble over her lips, and tried to ignore the band of longing winding around her heart. *Pick me for their mother.* She spluttered and almost spat water down her shirt. Where had that little gem come from? Having children meant getting married and *that* would never happen. 'Where's that waitress? I want to order lunch.'

Zac shook his head and looked around. He must've spotted someone who could help because he raised a hand and waved, before doing what she'd hoped he wouldn't. 'What about you? Obviously you'd want more than one child if you felt you'd missed out not having a sibling.'

She went for her standard reply, not prepared to reveal her deep but well-hidden longing that she barely acknowledged to herself. 'I've worked too hard to get where I am with my career to be taking time out for babies. Women I've talked to say that has set them back on the career pathway, and I'm not prepared to do that.'

Zac watched her, while behind those eyes she knew his brain would be working overtime. 'I don't buy it. That's the press-release version. What's the real story behind answering the same question you threw at me?'

He had a valid point. She hadn't minded asking him where he was headed on the subject of family, so she should be able to take it in return. Except she couldn't. They'd moved beyond the couple that used to have crazy sex all the time with no stopping for conversations. Now there was more between them they were learning about each other and she definitely liked the man she was getting to know. More than liked. But to reveal everything about her sorry upbringing was going too far. From years of learning to shut up those memories, they were now firmly locked away and she doubted the words were there. 'I—'

'Excuse me.' The waitress chose to arrive right then.

Phew. Not a reprieve but a few minutes to consider how to get around this without upsetting Zac and the easy way that had grown between them. Because *that* was important. She did not want to lose any ground they'd gained.

'Another water?' Zac asked.

'Yes, and I'll have the red snapper with salad.'

The waitress hadn't even turned away before Zac was saying, 'There's a question on the table, CC.'

Might as well get this over. 'I got Mum's undivided attention. She put all her love onto me. Except it was conditional and ugly.' Her sigh was bitter and very out of place in such a wonderful setting. 'Parenting takes special people and I'm not one of them.'

'Am I allowed to argue that point with you?' His voice was soft, gentle, almost a caress that said, *I'm here for you*.

'Afraid not. It's pointless.'

His mouth tightened. She'd hurt him.

Reaching for his hand, she said, 'I need to drop this, Zac. Seriously. I'm sorry if you think I don't trust you enough to talk about it. It's me I don't trust. My judgement about everything that happened in my family is warped and I'm just not ready to dissect it. I probably never will be, okay?'

His chin dipped in acknowledgement, though his eyes said he was still there for her if she changed her mind.

Squeezing those strong fingers that were curled around her hand, Olivia asked, 'Can we relax and make the most of sitting next to a sparkling pool on a tropical island? Leave the other stuff out of the picture?' She'd get down on her knees if that would help.

Zac leaned forward and placed his lips on her mouth. 'Yes,' he breathed as he kissed her.

As far as kisses went this one was tame, but it wound through her like a silky ribbon, touching, comforting, telling her that she wasn't alone with those deep fears any more. Had this Zac always been there? Should she have scratched the surface of him right back at the beginning, on that very first night they'd fallen into his bed, exhausted after making out in his lounge and still eager for more? No, she didn't think so. They would never have revealed anything about themselves back then. Talking hadn't fit the mix of what had made their affair so exciting. 'Thank you,' she murmured into his kiss.

They were interrupted with cutlery being placed on the table and the waitress asking if she could get them anything else while they waited for their meals.

'No, thanks.' Zac sat back, a smile tipping that gorgeous mouth upwards. His eyes locked on Olivia's. 'We've got everything we need.'

'The trevally are here,' Olivia called from the edge of the lawn in front of their bure an hour after they returned to Tokoriki.

Zac grabbed the fishing line and raced down to the

beach, calling at Olivia as he passed her, 'Watch this. I'm going to catch dinner.'

'You sure you weren't a caveman in a previous life?' She laughed.

'Weren't we all?' He unravelled the line and threw it as far as possible.

'I don't know. This whole "me man, me like hunting-gathering thing"—it's like men are born that way. I prefer going to a supermarket.'

Winding the line in as Donny had taught him, he grinned. 'The urge lurks below the skin, waiting for opportunities to show our women what wonderful providers and protectors we are.'

'So when women fish or hunt, what are they proving?'

'You've just flipped the argument. If I said that women are trying to prove they're as good as us I'd get my head knocked off, right?'

'I'll go and get my club.'

'Before you do, I admit that there are females who love all that outdoor activity as much as their menfolk, and some of them are very good at shooting deer or pig and catching a fish.'

A soft punch was delivered to his bicep. Olivia nodded along the beach. 'The score so far is locals three, visitor none.'

Zac tapped his chest with his fist. 'She wounds so easily.' He loved it when she was being cheeky and not considering every word before uttering it.

'If you can feel anything on the end of your line it's probably a pebble. There's your hook.' She peered at the water's edge, her grin wicked, making his toes curl with longing.

'This time.' He hurled the line out once more and began winding it back in.

'I don't think so,' Olivia said beside him.

'How do you know?'

Throw it out, bring it in. There was a timeless rhythm to this and, yes, he was enjoying fishing with the men.

'You've got another pebble.'

It took a second but he finally remembered where he was and what he was doing. 'This time,' he assured the disbelieving woman.

'Hey, Donny,' Olivia called. 'Zac's last fish must've been beginner's luck.'

Glancing over his shoulder, Zac nodded to the Fijian. 'Donny, don't listen to a word she says. I've got this.'

He was relieved the man had shown up. He and Olivia had agreed this might be the best place to talk to Donny about Josaia. Olivia had also suggested that he do the talking at first, man to man, so to speak.

Zac heard Olivia say, 'Hello, Josaia,' and his disappointment rose. They could not talk about surgery in front of the boy. Damn.

But Olivia had her ways. 'Josaia, can you help me find a shell to take home? One of those small conches would be good.' She waited for Josaia's reply, looking at him as she would any other child.

'I know where the best shells are.' He spoke hesitantly, as though expecting Olivia to withdraw from him any second.

'Cool. Let's go. Hopefully, by the time we get back Zac will have finally caught a fish.'

'Granddad catches them all the time.' Josaia bounced along beside Olivia, looking up at her so often he tripped over his own feet.

Donny watched them walk away. 'She's kind.'

'She is. She's also genuine.'

'I can see that. So can Josaia. He wouldn't have gone with her otherwise. He's learned to be wary of people's empty gestures.' Sadness lined Donny's statement.

Flicking the line out again, Zac said without preamble, 'You know we're doctors?'

'I wondered. Neither of you flinched when you saw Josaia, like you're used to seeing disfiguring scars.'

Zac was relieved. He'd thought he might've shown his feelings for the kid's predicament far too much. 'Olivia's a plastic surgeon.'

Donny turned to stare after his grandson again. 'What about you? Do you work in the same field?'

'I'm an orthopaedic surgeon.'

The man spun around to stare at him. 'Are you pulling my leg? Because if you are and my grandson learns…' He spluttered to a stop, unable to voice his anger.

Placing a hand on Donny's arm, Zac said, 'I am speaking the truth. We want to help Josaia.'

Donny gasped a few deep breaths, rubbed his forearm across his face. 'We don't have enough money. That's why our son-in-law works in Australia. He's trying to save for an operation for Josaia but…' Donny shook his head.

The line was getting into a tangle since Zac had stopped winding. Concentrating on sorting it out, he told the proud man, 'Let's start at the beginning and work from there. If it's okay with you, we'd like to look at Josaia's injuries and request copies of his medical records.'

His statement was met with silence. Could he have approached Donny differently? Might as well lay it all out. If he'd got it wrong then he had nothing to lose. 'We think it's probably best if Josaia has surgery in Auckland, where both of us practise.'

'You make it sound so easy.'

'I do know a thing or two about the New Zealand health system.'

Donny gripped Zac's hand. 'Thank you. I am glad you caught that trevally. It has brought my family much good luck.'

Zac grinned. 'Maybe that's why I haven't caught one today. There's only so much luck out there and we've used up our share for a while.'

Once Donny had talked with his wife and daughter, and explained everything to Josaia, he brought the lad to the bure.

'At the time of the accident we were told by a visiting doctor that plastic surgery would make the scar less visible and the lumps could be removed.'

'Has Josaia seen anyone else about this?'

'There aren't any plastic surgeons in Fiji. But, please, you can look today. Josaia likes you, he won't be a problem.'

'He found me a shell to take home.' She'd treasure it, as long as she could take it through quarantine at Auckland Airport. 'Hey, Josaia, can I touch your cheek?'

The boy nodded solemnly.

The muscle was tight and knobbly under her fingers. 'Open your mouth wide,' she instructed Josaia. Inside there was further scarring. 'I can do something to improve this.' She stepped back to allow Zac space.

'Josaia, show me how far you can move your arm,' Zac instructed.

Donny talked as his grandson moved his arm back and forth. 'It's tight. He can't move it far. Tendons were severed by the arrow of the gun and sewn back together shorter than before.'

'Will you make me better?' Josaia asked them, his eyes wide with hope.

Olivia answered, 'Would you like us to try?'

He nodded. 'Yes, please.'

'You would have to go to hospital again.'

'Will it hurt?'

Zac nodded. 'Yes, I'm sorry, but we'll give you something to stop most of the pain.'

Donny spoke quietly. 'I would like to accept your help, but how do we pay for this?'

Olivia wanted to wrap him in her arms and say *Don't worry, everything will be all right*, except she didn't want to trample on this family's pride. So she dodged some of the question. 'If we go ahead, would it be all right with you if we did the operations as a gift to Josaia?'

Donny blinked, ran a hand over his face. 'Why would you do that?'

'Part of what I like about being a doctor is helping people, giving them second chances, and Josaia deserves one.' Goodness, she'd be crying next.

Zac must've sensed her problem because he leaned closer so that his arm touched hers, and told Donny, 'Children shouldn't be disadvantaged because of someone else's mistake.'

'What can I say?' Donny asked in such a strangled voice Olivia smiled.

'You gave us a beautiful meal in your home. You might think there's no comparison but being welcomed into your house, meeting all your family, sharing that dinner with you was an experience we'll both remember for ever.' Now a tear did leak from the corner of Olivia's eye and trek down her face.

Donny reached for her hands, gripped them tight. 'Thank you so much. It's been hard, you know, watching my Josaia turn into a quiet, withdrawn version of himself. I will ring his father and tell him the good news. He'll be so happy.'

No pressure.

CHAPTER TWELVE

'THERE'S A BAND playing tonight,' Zac called from the outdoor shower box, where he was towelling himself dry.

'What sort of band?' Olivia asked from the bathroom, where she was apparently putting on her face.

Why she did that when her skin was clear and her face naturally beautiful he did not understand. But he knew not to say a word. 'It's a surprise.'

'Which means you have no idea.' She chuckled.

That sound, relaxed and happy, did things to him. Made him wish for more with Olivia: for a future, to be able to wake up every morning with her lying beside him, if not tangled around him. To know she'd be there for him, day in day out, and that he'd have her back all the time would be amazing. Right. Not that he didn't have her back already, but sometimes he didn't know what he was protecting her from.

'Something like that,' he agreed, as he wrapped the towel around his waist and headed into the main room. 'Anything from locals to visiting rock stars. I heard a whisper about two guys and their guitars.'

Olivia leaned around the corner, her hair swinging over her arm, her face lit up with a big smile. 'That narrows the options.'

'Better than bongo drums at any rate.'

She just laughed and disappeared back into the bathroom.

If only they weren't going to dinner but staying here, checking out that enormous bed for what it was intended. He was done playing Mr Nice Guy on the far side. While wonderful, the spooning hadn't been enough, more a teaser of what could have been. Pulling on a shirt, he sighed. One more night. Tomorrow they would fly out of here in a float plane, headed for the airport. This had been a fabulous few days. Continuing to get to know each other seemed the way forward.

'I heard that there's going to be lobster on the menu tonight.' Olivia bounced into the room, her hands busy slipping earrings into her lobes.

His hands faltered, stopped, buttons ignored. 'You look stunning.'

The red dress she'd somehow squeezed into accentuated all those lovely curves to perfection.

'You think?' She spun around on her tiptoes. 'Not my usual style.'

Her cleavage had never been so—so... His mouth dried. The back of the dress—there wasn't any. Nothing worth mentioning anyway. Was it really a dress when there was hardly any more fabric than in the blue and lime-green bikini she'd lounged around in all day? The hemline barely made it onto her thighs. 'So not you.'

Her smile dipped. 'Should I change?'

Zac's heart stopped. He stepped across the gap between them, caught her hands in his, and tugged her close. Not so close that they were touching. Then they'd never go to dinner. But close enough that he could breathe in her scent. 'I have never seen you look so, so beautiful. Ravishing. And before you go thinking you're not beautiful all the time, you absolutely are. I'm going to order you more dresses like that.'

'You say the nicest things.' Her smile was back. 'I've always wanted to go all out and wear something like this but don't often have the courage. That creation I wore on the night of the gala was the first in a long time. You make me feel it's okay, so for a moment there I got a bit worried.'

'I'm a bloke. Clear and concise speech isn't one of my strong points.' He dropped her hands. He needed to finish dressing if they were ever going to head to the restaurant.

But one button done up and Olivia was laughing at him. 'Let me.' She undid the button, realigned his shirt front and started over. Her fingers were light as they worked down his shirt. Over his chest. Down to his abs—which were sucking in on themselves and just about touching his spine.

Zac gritted his teeth, and his hands clenched at his sides. She was killing him. Cell by damned cell.

'Relax,' she said in a low, throaty growl.

Oh, right. Sure. Easy as. He took an unsteady step back and snatched up his trousers from the bed, and muttered, 'Relax, she says.'

Olivia did wicked without even trying. Her mouth curved into a sumptuous smile, her eyes widened with promise as she slapped her hands on those slim hips. 'How soon can you get me those new dresses? I never knew wearing something so simple could have this effect on a man.' Her eyes widened even further, her smile grew bigger. 'Not just any man either.'

'There is nothing simple about you or your damned dress.'

'Damned dress, huh?' Her gaze cruised down his

body, pausing at his obvious reaction to that piece of fabric that was in danger of being torn off her. 'This is our last night.'

Squeezing his eyes shut, he counted to ten, slowly. Nothing changed. He continued to twenty. His blood still pulsed throughout his body, heating every cell it touched. Finally he drew a shaky breath and locked eyes with her before growling, 'Last night, last cocktail and final dinner under the palms, last of everything to do with our holiday.'

Last of that stupid ban on sex. Whoa, did that mean they could get up close and personal tomorrow? As soon as they landed back in Auckland could they go straight to his apartment? Or her house? He didn't care which as long as he could scratch this itch.

Olivia just laughed and picked up a pair of red shoes with heels that would be lethal if flung at a guy. 'Let's go enjoy ourselves.'

At least she had the sense not to hold his hand or slip her arm through his as they walked along the path to the restaurant. If she had Zac doubted his ability not to swing her up into his arms and run back to their bure. Last evening or not.

'We've been given the best table.' Olivia glanced around the outdoor dining area as she sank onto the chair being held out for her by their waiter. The table was set well back from everyone else with hibiscus growing on three sides, soft light from lanterns making it feel as though they were in a bubble. A very cosy bubble.

Zac blinked. Was he still trying to get his libido under control? 'Maybe it's our turn.'

Every other night honeymooners had sat here. She and Zac didn't have that qualification. 'I feel special.'

'What can I get you to drink?' the waiter asked.

Zac didn't ask her what she preferred, instead rattled off the name of the best champagne on the wine list. 'We're celebrating,' he told her when the young man had gone.

'Celebrating?'

'Anything and everything.' He leaned forward, those dark eyes suddenly serious. 'I haven't had such a wonderful holiday, ever. Thank you.'

Her eyes filled with unexpected tears. 'I didn't do anything.' *Except tease the hell out of you back in the bure.*

'Exactly. You were just you, and I'd never met that you before.'

A tear escaped. Then another. She quickly lifted her glass of water to her lips. What was with this crying stuff? She was usually stronger than that.

'You're supposed to reciprocate, tell me how you've discovered a superman.'

Then the champagne arrived. 'Compliments of management,' the waitress told them.

'This isn't anything to do with Josaia?' Zac asked.

A huge smile split the woman's face. 'Enjoy your evening.'

When Olivia had a glass in her hand she raised it to Zac. 'To us and our fabulous holiday.' This experience had loosened a lot of permanent knots inside her. She and Zac had gelled so well she was even wondering if it might be possible to have a life together in some way. She wanted to ask if they might continue seeing each other back in Auckland, but the old warning bells rattled in her skull, putting a dampener on that. *Just enjoy tonight and wait for tomorrow to unfold.* But she didn't do waiting to see what happened. That meant no control.

Zac tapped his glass on hers. 'We haven't finished yet. Our plane doesn't leave until ten in the morning.'

'Okay, to the rest of our stay in paradise.' Excitement shimmied down her spine. One more night. Dinner under the stars, maybe some dancing if the band of two turned out to be halfway decent, a stroll on the beach after ditching her heels, and then... Then she planned on seducing Zac into using that enormous bed for something other than spooning.

Those picks Olivia called shoes swung from one of her hands while she held onto him firmly with the other. 'There's something about walking on sand at night.' Her voice was a murmur, drifting on the warm, still air, encasing Zac in tenderness.

The need he'd barely been holding onto spilled through him, hissed out between them. It would not be contained any more. After days of bikinis and figure-hugging dresses, laughter and fun, he had to have Olivia—in his arms, under his body. He ached to fill her, to kiss her senseless. But there was that damned rule. He would not be the one to break it. He'd given his word. Never again was he going to make a promise. About anything. Tugging his hand free, Zac went for flippant. Only way to go. 'Who wouldn't love damp sand between their toes, scratchy and irritating? Wonderful stuff.'

Olivia's laughter was so carefree it tugged at his heart. She glanced down at their bare feet and dropped her shoes. 'Come on, then. Let's wash the sand off.' And in a flash her dress was being flung onto the sand beside those red picks. 'Coming?'

'You're such a tease, Olivia Coates-Clark,' Zac growled, even as he tore his shirt over his head. Talk about upping the ante. His failing self-control would never cope, and yet he followed her towards the sea, nearly falling flat on his face as he ran down the beach while trying to step out of his trousers at the same time.

Plunging into the warm water, he swam towards Olivia, who seemed to be treading water too far out. 'Hey,' he growled. 'Stop right there.'

'Or what?' She laughed and began swimming away.

Zac poured on the speed and quickly caught her, catching her around the waist and pulling her to him. 'Or I'll have to kiss you senseless.' She felt good. That compact, smooth body slip-sliding against his. Cranking up his lust. As if that was hard to do.

Salty lips covered his, and her tongue exploded into his mouth. Her hands gripped his head, holding him to her. This was no soft, sweet kiss. This was CC giving her all. This was what he needed. His hands were on her butt, lifting her higher up his body, across his reaction to her. Without breaking the kiss, she wound her legs around his waist and hovered over his throbbing need.

Twisting his mouth away from those lips, he croaked, 'No sex, babe.'

'Stupid rule. I'm breaking it.' Low and sexy laughter highlighted her intent.

Relief nearly dumped him underwater. Words dried in his mouth. So he went back to kissing while trying to hold Olivia and shove his boxers down his thighs all at once.

Suddenly a small hand pressed between them, her fingers splayed on his chest. 'Wait.'

'Wait?' His voice was hoarse with longing. If she'd changed her mind he'd lose his permanently.

'That massive bed. The bure. The Fijian experience. I want that.'

This time relief had Zac sinking into the water, taking Olivia with him, so that she sat over his point of desire. 'Since when have we been one-act-per-night types?'

Her answer was to slide over him, taking him deep within her, her head tipped back, her body quivering as she came fast. Four nights of restraining himself exploded in one deep thrust into her heat.

Dragging themselves up the beach, they scooped up their clothes and, holding hands, raced to the bure. *Except I'm not running.* Olivia grinned. *I'm skipping. I am over the moon with happiness.* 'What a goddamned waste. Four nights and we didn't do it. Are we idiots or what?'

Zac swung their hands high. 'There are plenty of words out there we could use, but I'd rather concentrate on getting you to beg me to make love to you in that bed we've been pretending we haven't shared.'

'Good answer.' Her shoes and dress slipped out of her hand at the doors leading inside. 'Let's hit the shower first. I don't usually season my sex with salt.'

'The outside shower.'

'Is there any other?' A quick sluice off and she dried Zac as he fumbled with a towel to do the same with her. Impatient, she tossed the towels aside and grabbed his hand, pulled him into the main room and leapt into the bed, taking him with her so that they tumbled into a heap of arms and legs. Not that Zac had needed any persuasion. He was already showing interest in her, in the way only men could.

Goddamn. She grinned and shook herself. This had to be the most wonderful, magical, fabulous way to end their stay on the island. Maybe waiting those long, tension-filled nights had been the way to go, had added to the tension and wound up the orgasmic relief. 'Zac,' she whispered. 'Long and slow.' As she trailed kisses over his chest she continued, 'We've got all night.'

'Yeah, babe, not leaving until ten tomorrow.'

Some time after four in the morning, as the sun began to lighten the bure around the edges, Olivia snuggled her exhausted body against Zac's and traced a line across his chest with a fingertip.

'This is unlike other times for us.'

'Yeah, you're talking too much, for one thing.'

'I feel different. I guess lying in bed together afterwards has something to do with that.' In fact, she was shocked at how much she was enjoying lying here with Zac, knowing neither of them would shortly leap out of bed and head home, or to work, or anywhere. 'This is taking it to a whole new level.' As if there was a depth to making out with Zac she'd never known before. She should be scared. She wasn't. Not right this moment, with Zac's body wrapped around hers and her muscles feeling deliciously sated.

The hands that had been working their magic on her back stopped moving. 'Regret not zapping that rule earlier?'

Locking gazes with him, her heart pounded at a ridiculous rate. He didn't look unhappy about what she'd said, more cautious. 'Not at all.' Having fun doing other things together had added more to their relationship. 'I have had the most amazing holiday with you.' *I want to have more of them.*

'Aw, shucks.' He pulled the sheet up to their necks. 'You say the nicest things. In case you're wondering, I've had a wonderful time doing some great things with you too. Now let's fall asleep in each other's arms for the last few hours of our holiday.'

Yep, soon reality would return in the form of Auckland, work and her mother. And in thinking where to go with this new relationship with Zac. Her eyelids drooped shut. She would not think about that now. Not when his strong arms held her as though she was delicate. Not when she could breathe in the scent of their lovemaking and Zac's aftershave. Not when... She drifted into a dream-laden sleep filled with images of the man sharing the bed.

Josaia and all his family were standing on the beach when Zac and Olivia turned up to board their float plane.

Olivia hugged Lauan. 'I'm so glad we met you and your family.'

Lauan was crying openly and shaking her head. 'No, it is us who are glad.'

'We'll be in touch very soon, I promise.' Leaving these wonderful people wasn't as easy as she'd expected. Zac nudged her out of the way to have his turn hugging Lauan. 'We'll schedule Josaia's surgeries as soon as possible.' He was repeating what they'd all discussed yesterday afternoon.

Donny stepped up and said, 'Josaia has something for you both.'

'Dr Zac, this is for you.' The boy handed over a bright blue *sulu* with all the gravity of a ceremony for royalty.

Zac took the carefully folded cotton cloth that Fijian men traditionally wore tied around their waists at special times.

Josaia stepped in front of Olivia. 'This is yours.'

She dropped to her knees and wrapped her arms around Josaia, a yellow *sulu* that could be wrapped around her body like a strapless dress in her hand. 'Thank you so much. I'll look after it, I promise.'

Once inside the plane Olivia leaned forward to wave goodbye. Suddenly the plane was racing and bumping across the sea and finally lifting into the sky.

She'd had the most amazing five days, and now she didn't know what was ahead. Hope rose, hope for a future they could share. The hope backed off. She couldn't make a full commitment to Zac. Her mother made sure of that. There just wasn't enough of herself to go round. She wasn't going to try to spread herself too thin. That's how people got hurt.

Zac lifted her hand and kissed her knuckles. 'Stop overthinking things.'

Did he know what was going on in her mind? Of course not. He didn't know the half of what went on in her life.

She gripped his hand and turned to stare outside, absorbing every last moment of Fiji.

Olivia shivered as she clambered out of the taxi outside her house. 'Why does the weather have to be wet and cold tonight of all nights?' she grumbled.

Zac only laughed. 'Bringing us back to earth with a thump, isn't it?'

Grabbing her case, she ran for the shelter of her covered veranda. That's when she noticed lights on inside. Then the steady beat of music reached her. And her stomach dived. *No. Not tonight. Not when I'm so happy.*

'You going to open that door?' Zac asked.

Not while you're here. She waved frantically at the taxi driver. He had to take Zac away. Now. Not after that coffee she'd suggested when they'd turned into her street. 'Wait,' she yelled.

'Too late,' Zac muttered. 'You don't want me coming in after all?'

'I've got a headache.'

Zac dropped his case and reached for her. 'That sudden? I'm picking it's because there's someone inside you don't want me to meet.' His hands were gentle on her upper arms, his thumbs rubbing back and forth in a coaxing manner. 'I thought we were better than that, had moved on from the quick visits to something more real.'

So did I, until reality slapped me around the ears. She'd been an idiot to think there was a way around the problem on the other side of her front door. 'I'm sorry.' She didn't want his sympathy—or worse, was afraid of seeing a look of horror in his eyes when he saw how far gone her mother would be.

The sound of her front door being unlocked sent a wave of panic through her. 'You have to go. Now.'

'Olivia, darling, there you are. I've been wondering where you'd got to and when you'd be back. They wouldn't tell me anything at the hospital.'

Olivia was a dab hand at interpreting the alcohol-laden slur. One glance at Zac and she knew he was also right up to speed on the situation. Anger—at her mother, at Zac for learning her truth—rolled up and spilled out. 'Mum, what are you doing here? You know I don't like you in my house when I'm away.'

A firm hand on her arm stopped her diatribe. 'Olivia, it's okay.'

'No, it's not. You don't get it. This is my mother, Cindy Coates-Clark. Mum, meet Zachary Wright, a friend—' No, damn it. 'Zac and I have been in Fiji together. We have had a wonderful time and now we'd like to wind down from our flight home. Alone.'

'Pleased to meet you, Zachary. Call me Cindy.' A wave of alcohol fumes wafted between them all.

Her mother stepped back and held the door wide, as though it was her place to do so. 'Do come in.'

'Thank you, Cindy.' Zac picked up the cases and nodded Olivia through in front of him. 'I'll leave mine just inside the door while we have that coffee.'

'You still want it?' When she locked her eyes with his, he nodded.

'Yes.' Like there was nothing out of the ordinary, being greeted by a scantily clad woman who was obviously plastered.

Heavy black smudges of mascara covered Cindy's cheeks, and bright red lipstick had run into the lines around her mouth. Her low-cut top revealed way too much cleavage, and her skirt...

Olivia gulped as anger and disappointment again boiled over. 'Mum, that was a new suit. I haven't even worn it.' And never would now that three-quarters of the skirt had been hacked off. She'd been thrilled when she'd found the emerald-coloured outfit at her favourite shop.

'It's far sexier now. You can be so old-fashioned with your clothes, darling.'

'I wonder why.' From the day she'd turned thirteen her mother had spent a fortune on buying her clothes that had made her feel uncomfortable even around the cat, let alone the kids she'd hung out with. Humiliating didn't begin to describe it.

Now Zac was seeing things she never wanted him to know about. 'Zac, about that coffee...'

'I'll make it, shall I?' He hid his disgust very well. 'Would you like a coffee, Cindy?'

'Coffee? I don't think so. Why don't you two join me with a gin? Zac, I know you'd like one. You're a real man. Not like—'

'Mum, stop it. Now. We are not having gin.' She stepped into the kitchen and crumpled. *Welcome home, Olivia. Welcome back to life as you really know it.* Empty bottles lay everywhere. Half-full takeout food containers covered the bench, dirty cutlery and glasses filled the spaces. 'How long have you been here?'

'I don't know. Days?' Mum sounded confused all of a sudden.

Strong arms wound around Olivia, held her from dropping in a heap. 'Hey, we'll get it sorted.' Zac's low voice was full of compassion and wove around her like the comfort blanket she'd taken everywhere with her as a toddler. 'You're not alone, okay?'

Yes, she was. Her mother was her problem. This had nothing to do with Zac, and never would. Despite the warmth that stole through her at his words. She stayed in the circle of his arms—just for one more minute. Her chin rested on his chest. One minute, then she'd toughen up and face the consequences of having gone away without telling her mother where she was.

Finally she stepped away, put space between her and Zac. 'You have to go.'

Frustration deepened his voice. 'No, Olivia, I don't. I'm with you, at your side, looking out for you.'

On her phone she found the taxi company number and stabbed the button. Forcing a toughness she didn't feel on her face, she snapped, 'I'm not asking, I'm telling you to go.' Someone from the taxi company answered and she rattled off directions, ended the call. 'They'll be five minutes.'

He gave no further argument, just kissed her softly. 'Good night, sweetheart. Talk to you in the morning.'

'No, Zac. Don't. It's over. We're done. Permanently.' It was the only way forward for her.

But when the front door had closed behind him Olivia leaned against the hall wall and felt her heart crack into pieces. It had taken this for her to realise her hope for the future with Zac was actually love for Zac. She wanted to be with him, to give him so much, to share a life. To openly show him her love. To try to be the woman she hadn't thought she could be. But that mess in her kitchen told her otherwise. Dreams were fairytales.

Sliding down the wall, she wrapped her arms around her legs, dropped her head on her knees, and let the tears come. She hadn't cried over her mother for so long but there was no stopping the torrent. For a brief time she'd let hope into her heart, had wanted more with Zac. How dumb could she get? This had always been going to happen. Therefore, the sooner the better. Now she could move on, without Zac, and do what she'd always done—survive and look out for her mother.

Zac stared at Olivia's house until the taxi turned the corner at the end of the street. His throat was dry, his heartbeat slow and his gut knotted tight. What a difference twenty-four hours made. From sexy and fun in that red dress to heartbroken at home, it was like Olivia had flipped from one person to another.

Now he understood so much. The control she constantly maintained over herself and everything around her was a coping mechanism.

There'd be no controlling her mother.

Olivia didn't want to be like her mother.

The glimpse of worry when he'd said that dress was so different from what he was used to seeing her in now made sense.

'Well, hello, you're nothing like your mum.' Despite having spent only a few minutes with Cindy and not knowing anything about her, he knew Olivia was the polar opposite from her mother.

But you didn't have to kick me out like I mean nothing to you.

When Olivia had mentioned her mother was an alcoholic he'd had no idea what that meant in real terms. Drunk and disorderly didn't cover it. Cindy whined like a spoilt brat, created chaos. She'd helped herself to her daughter's clothes, ruining them in the process. Helped herself to the house, the contents of the kitchen, and trashed it as only belligerent teenagers did. What had that woman done to Olivia's life? Her sense of belonging, her future?

The resignation in CC's eyes had hit him hard. She was responsible for that woman, and he knew all about responsibility. He'd learned it the hard way. Hopefully Olivia hadn't, but deep down he knew this situation went a long way to explaining why she ran solo.

You don't have to be alone any more.

Olivia wasn't made for that. She was loving, caring, sharing, and a whole load more.

The taxi pulled up in Quay Street. His apartment building loomed above, dark and unwelcoming. He'd rather be back at Olivia's house, no matter the mess inside. He wasn't thinking about the state of the kitchen.

But you sent me away, Olivia. Again.

As Zac rode the elevator to his floor a slow burn began in his belly. He'd been shoved out of Olivia's life for a second time. She hadn't given him a chance to stay, to talk about it, to do any damned thing except get out of her life. What had their holiday been about if not learning more about each other and getting closer?

Learning that I love you, Olivia. Do you know that? Do you know I've broken all my rules for you? That for the first time ever I'm seeing a future that's got people in it—you and our children.

The doors slid apart but Zac didn't move. The itch had gone.

The doors began closing. Sticking his foot in the gap so they opened again, Zac hoisted his bag and dragged his feet towards his apartment. He'd pour a whisky and try to fathom where to go from here.

How damned typical that when he'd finally fallen in love he wasn't wanted.

CHAPTER THIRTEEN

'DON'T HANG UP, OLIVIA.' Zac didn't give her time to say hello. 'This is about Josaia.'

'I'm listening.' Olivia could listen to him all day, but of course she'd spent the last ten days doing her damnedest to push him away, out of her head, her heart. She missed him so much it was unbelievable. It was like her heart and mind were stuck in Fiji mode with Zac, talking and laughing, while her real life was grinding along without any joy.

'Theatre's booked at the private hospital for Saturday morning. I've managed to inveigle a free bed for four nights so we're set to go.' Zac sounded upbeat and pleased with himself. As he should be. He'd been hassling everyone he knew to get Josaia's surgery organised. All the staff assisting were doing it gratis. No surprise there. When Zac wanted to he could charm the grumpiest of old men into putting his hand in his pocket and handing over his life savings.

'You should start a charity organisation for kids like Josaia,' Olivia acknowledged.

'*I* should? You're the one who knows how to pull at people's heartstrings. Look at how successful Andy's gala night turned out to be.'

Had she pulled Zac's heartstrings? Ever? Even a

teeny-weeny bit? Why was she wondering when a yes only added to her grief? Staying away from him was hard enough already. She only talked to him about Josaia's upcoming surgery, cutting him off the moment he started on about anything personal. 'I'll see you at the motel at five.' They'd decided between themselves to pay for a motel unit for the family close to the hospital. Zac was picking up Josaia and his family from the airport later in the day. Tomorrow they had a free day, and then it would be D-day.

'You could come with me.'

'I've got a clinic starting at two.'

Zac sighed, his upbeat mood gone. 'Promise me you'll be at the motel. It's important for Josaia.'

She didn't make promises. Her word was usually enough. 'I promise.' *I do?*

'Are you sure you're not a secret needleworker?' Zac asked from the other side of the operating table on Saturday. 'You're so patient, creating delicate stitches even where the outcome won't be visible to anyone.'

Olivia glanced up at him, her heart stuttering when his dark eyes locked on hers. 'I could've taken up knitting.'

'That'd be messy.' He grinned. She mightn't be able to see his mouth behind that mask but his eyes were light and sparkling.

Olivia concentrated on her patient. She'd reopened the wound that ran down the side of Josaia's face and removed tissue causing lumps where the previous stitches had been pulled too tight. Now she was painstakingly suturing layer after layer, careful with each and every stitch. While it was what everyone saw on the outside that upset Josaia, she could make it so much better by preparing the underneath muscle properly.

'You want to close the shoulder wound once I've worked on Josaia's shoulder?' Zac asked. 'We might as well go for broke and have everything looking as close to new as possible.'

'Make those kids want their friend back.'

Kay looked up from her monitors. 'I hope Josaia tells them where to go.'

'I suspect he might after this,' Zac told the anaesthetist. 'He's been different ever since we said we could operate. Hopeful, expectant. Which puts the pressure on us.'

Olivia clipped the end of her last suture and straightened her back. 'There you go, young man. As good as new.'

Zac swapped places with Olivia. It was his turn to set things right for Josaia. 'Let's hope I can do the same. At least no one gets to see what I do.' He picked up a scalpel.

'They will on the outside. It will be great to see Josaia with his confidence back, swimming and diving with the best of them.'

'I hope he finds some new friends. He doesn't need the old ones.' Olivia swabbed as Zac made incisions. 'But I guess Josaia doesn't have a lot of choice on the island.'

'It must be hell for his family, seeing how he's treated. No parent would want their child to suffer like that.' Zac exposed the collarbone, where it had been broken. 'Re-breaking this is kind of awful. The kid's going to be in pain for a while.'

'Think about how those pins you're going to put in will help him. One day he'll appreciate it.' The sooner the better if the boy was to make a full recovery with friends and school.

'Right, let's get this done.' He reached for the first pin.

As soon as the surgeries were completed and Josaia was wheeled away to Recovery, Olivia and Zac went to put the family at ease.

Then they headed for the car park and Zac suggested lunch downtown. 'We could go to the Viaduct.'

'Sorry, Zac, but I'm not hungry.' She'd eaten very little over the last couple of days, food making her feel nauseous.

'What's going on, Olivia? Don't give me the "nothing" reply. I won't believe you.'

The steel in his tone overwhelmed her. She could feel her body being pulled towards him. It would be so easy to lean in and let go of her problem for a while. The thing with that was that her mother wasn't going to go away; would be there causing havoc when she finally took up the reins again. Tightening her spine, she told him, 'I have an appointment in an hour, and before that I need to hit the supermarket.' Though why when she wasn't eating she had no idea. That had just dropped into her head when she was trying to sound convincing to Zac.

'An appointment with who?' Of course he went for the important part of her statement.

'A lawyer, a psychologist, and a cop,' she blurted, close to unravelling. Had to be why she'd answered with the truth. She needed to get away from Zac fast, before she became a blithering idiot and spilled her guts all over his classy leather jacket.

Where was her car key? Scrabbling around in the bottom of her bag didn't produce it. Tipping the contents onto the bonnet of her car, she couldn't believe it wasn't there. Great. Just great.

'This what you're looking for?' Zac swung a key from his finger.

Snatching it from him, she began throwing everything back in her bag. 'Where did you find it?'

'Where are you meeting these people?'

'At home.' She bent to pick up her wallet from where it had slipped onto the tarmac.

'I'll drive you. Come on.' He took her elbow.

She tugged free. 'I can drive myself. Anyway, I can't leave my car here.'

Zac's hand was back on her arm. 'You can and you will. I'm taking you home, Olivia.'

That got her. Slap bang in her heart. She didn't pull away. She couldn't. She needed Zac, and, as frightening as that was, she went with the desperate longing to have someone at her side. 'Next you'll be telling me you're coming to the meeting.' Geez, had she just said that with hope in her voice?

'I'll make the coffee.'

He did more than that. Even when she nodded at the door for him to leave he stayed and listened as the horrible facts about her mother were aired and discussion began on what to do about Cindy. The truth was that there wasn't a lot that could be done unless her mother committed to a programme and went into care. Her latest hideous deed, arrested for driving while drunk on Thursday, made Olivia's stomach churn, and when she lifted her eyes to Zac's she fully expected to see total disgust all over his face. But no. His hand engulfed her shaking ones, his thumb rubbed back and forth over her fingers, and his eyes were full of understanding.

Olivia *needed* to leap up and drag Zac to her front

door, push him out, and lock it behind him. She *wanted* him here with her, holding her hand as he was. Split right down the middle, her emotions were raw and out of control. She aimed to do what she always did when this happened and focus on her mother's current situation. But it wasn't working. The words were going in but they weren't registering as clearly as they should.

By the time the meeting was over she was as aware as ever that her mother was a ticking time bomb and unwilling to take charge of herself. It had been suggested Olivia walk away, make her mother face up to her situation, but she didn't think she could do that. It would go against everything she believed in. Even now, when she was fighting Zac's pull, fighting this deep, paralysing need to let him into her life, she had to hold on to the only way she knew how to cope with her mother—by standing strong, alone.

Shutting the front door behind the lawyer, she leaned back against it, closing her eyes. Did she even have the energy to make it to the kitchen where Zac was waiting? She had to tell him to leave. It was getting to be a habit.

'Hey,' Zac said from somewhere in front of her. 'You need to go to bed and get some shut-eye.'

'I have to check Josaia's doing okay.'

'I'm going to head in there shortly so I can let you know if there's anything you need to deal with. I spoke to the ward sister while you were showing that lot out and she says he's doing fine. The family are with him.' Zac draped an arm over her shoulders and led her down the hallway in the direction of her bedroom. 'When did you last sleep properly?'

'I have no idea.'

'Get into bed and I'll make you a hot chocolate.'

Olivia sank onto the edge of her bed. 'Hot chocolate? I haven't had one of those in years.' *Since I had measles and Dad looked after me.* Huh? Dad had done that? Yeah, he had, just as he'd once spent lots of time with her. Before he'd got jaded and bitter about Mum, and had made another life.

Zac pulled her to her feet again. 'No, you don't. Let's get you into your PJs first.' He began unbuttoning her shirt and it was nothing like last time when he'd made her body hot with need. This loving gesture filled her heart with gladness and relief.

'I'll manage.' Her fingers worked the zip on her trousers. When Zac reached her door she called, 'Hey, you. Thank you for…everything.'

He came back and kissed her on each cheek. 'Told you I was here for you.'

Scary. 'Zac, I don't do being looked after.' Deep, deep breath. 'You have to go. You have to stay gone this time. Please.' Her voice cracked over the lump of tears clogging her throat.

Zac shrugged. 'Here's the thing. I don't do walking away from someone I care about either.'

Had Zac just said he cared about her? No, he couldn't have. She must be asleep already, having a dream. At least it wasn't a nightmare.

Zac let himself out of Olivia's house and made sure the door locked behind him. With a bit of luck Olivia would sleep right through until tomorrow. One thing for certain was that she needed to.

It was about the only thing he was sure of, he thought as he climbed into his vehicle and slammed the door against the light rain. That, and the fact she wouldn't be letting him back into her house tomorrow morning.

Looking up the path to her house, he recalled some of the comments made by the lawyer, and wondered just what sort of childhood Olivia must've had with a mother so far off the rails. What woman wanted to dress up as her daughter's lookalike? Wanted to hang out with a bunch of giggly teens? One eyebrow rose. Olivia a giggly teen? Hard to imagine.

Slowly pulling away, he kept going over everything he'd heard about Cindy Coates-Clark. How cruel of Olivia's father to leave her to deal with her alcoholic mother, especially when she'd been so young.

Toot, toot. A quick glance in the rear-view mirror showed a truck up his boot. He waved. 'Sorry, mate.' And planted his foot, roaring away from the corner.

He'd go see Josaia, then head home for the night. Tomorrow morning he'd take breakfast to Olivia's house.

Think that's going to win you entrance to her lair, do you?

No, not a sod's chance, but he had to try, if only to show her he wasn't repelled by anything he'd heard today. If anything, he was more determined to be a part of her life. At the moment he'd take the crumbs, but he fully intended to win her over completely so they'd have a future together.

His hand clenched, banged the steering wheel. Damn—families could be such screw-ups. He and Olivia had got the pick of them. What was Mark like as a father? Did he show his boys he loved them? Would he blame them for everything or walk out of their lives when the going got tough? And if he did, who would be there for them?

I would. But he didn't know the boys. Not really. Only one way to rectify that. But he and Mark didn't get along. *So go fix that. Start at the beginning and get to know your brother again, learn to put the angst behind you and love him as you always did, always have.*

Olivia rolled over onto her back and stared up at the ceiling. The sunlit ceiling.

'What time is it?'

Eight thirty-five, according to the screen on her phone.

She'd missed a load of texts while in the land of nod, starting last night.

Josaia says hi to Dr Olivia. He's doing fine and can't wait to be up and running around, despite the pain. Hope you're sleeping and don't get this till the morning. Hugs, Zac.

Thinking of you, and wishing we were back on Tokoriki enjoying dinner under the palm trees. More hugs, Zac.

Hitting the sack now. See you in the morning.

No, you won't. I've got a mother to sort out, and wounds to lick.

Outside your door with breakfast.

Had Zac knocking on the door been what had woken her? Olivia leapt out of bed and headed down the hall.

Wait up. You're going to let Zac in? Think about this. Is it wise when you're going to walk away from him again? It's not fair on him to be running hot and cold all the time. Either let him into your life or cut all ties—now.

Her feet dragged as she turned for the kitchen and

the kettle. Strong coffee was needed. Her heart was so slow it was in danger of stopping. She didn't want Zac gone but what else could she do? She had nothing to offer him.

She loved Zac. She knew it bone deep. He was the one for her. *Sniff.* But she wasn't right for him. Never would be.

With two coffees on board and a hot shower having washed away the sleep sludge on her skin, Olivia headed out her front door to see Josaia, and tripped over a paper bag with a takeout logo on it. Breakfast. Gluggy cold pancakes, bacon, and maple syrup filled the container she opened. 'Oh, Zac, you're making this so hard for me.'

She dropped the bag into her rubbish bin and headed for her garage, only remembering when the door rolled open that her car was still in the hospital's car park. Back inside the house she changed her shoes. Walking to the hospital would help clear her head.

Maybe.

Josaia was arguing with Donny about getting out of bed when Olivia arrived at his room. 'I don't like staying in bed.'

'You have to wait until Dr Olivia's checked you over,' his grandfather growled.

'If Josaia's that keen to get up then there's no reason why he shouldn't,' Olivia told them.

Josaia grinned. 'See?' But when he moved pain filled his face and he stopped.

'Take it slowly.' Olivia spoke firmly. 'I need to look at your face first. Then you'd better be careful what you do until Dr Zac sees you.' She needed to get out of

there before he turned up and started asking why she
hadn't returned any of his messages.

'He came when I was asleep.' Josaia slowly sat up,
his damaged cheek turned up to her. 'My face is better, isn't it?'

If he could think that with a line of stitches running
down his cheek then he was well on the way to recovery. 'Lots better.'

'My friends are going to like me again.'

Thud. Olivia's heart sank. 'Josaia, you are still going
to have a scar, just not as obvious and no more lumps
and bumps.'

'My arm's going to work properly.'

'Soon, yes. You have to do a lot of work first, ex-
ercises that Dr Zac will show you.' But those friends?
'Let's take everything slowly, eh?' She sat down beside him and turned his head so that the overhead light
shone on the wound. No redness or puffiness, just a neat
line that would heal into a thin, flat scar that over time
would fade to a pale mark on his skin. 'That's looking
good.' Pride filled her. Hopefully she'd made this boy's
life a little easier.

If only her mother was as easily pleased when she
visited later.

'I am not going into one of those rehab places. They're
full of pious do-gooders who think having a drink is
a crime.'

Clocked driving at eighty-five Ks per hour in a res-
idential area while drunk was a crime. 'You're lucky
Judge Walters has given you another chance to fix your
life. He's ordered you to go into a clinic. If you don't
you'll appear before him again and this time he'll throw
the book at you. You already have one drunk-driving

conviction.' She drew in a breath. 'I've made you an appointment for tomorrow at the clinic in Remuera. I'll come with you.'

'Bet that man you went away with wouldn't do anything naughty, like having a drink too many.'

Olivia sighed at her mother's classic tactic of changing the subject. 'Leave Zac out of this.'

'Why? You got the hots for him?'

I don't want him sullied by you. 'We're friends, nothing more.' *Nothing less either. If only...*

'He's cocky, thinks he's every woman's gift.' Her mother looked smug as she raised her coffee to her lips, then put it down without a sip.

'No, Mum, he does not.' Confident, comfortable in his own skin, but not cocky.

'You watch. He'll get what he wants from you and walk away. He's not the settling-down type.'

Mum always aimed for the bull's-eye. Never missed either. 'You know an awful lot about Zac for having spent very little time with him.'

'He's going to hurt you, darling. Trust me, I know men and how they operate. You are fair game with this one.'

She snapped, 'Zac is not like you think. You're insulting him with your accusations.'

'Watch this space,' her mother drawled, before changing tactics again. 'Darling, I'm only thinking of you. I don't want to see you get hurt. I know what that's like, believe me.'

'Why are you doing this? You want to destroy everything I hold dear.'

'Ha, you care about him. Knew it. I worry about what happens to you. I'm your mother, I want you to be happy.' Her hands shook so badly coffee slopped onto the table.

Mum's frightened. Of what? She's been going on about Zac. Aha. Got it. She's afraid she'll have to share me. She's always done this. She drove Dad away, pushed friends out of my life, and I've gone along with it, believing I can't love two people at once, can't be there for anyone but her.

'Goddamn,' she said under her breath. *Have I been wrong?* 'Mum, I've got to go. I'll pick you up at ten tomorrow.'

'Come back, Olivia. I need to talk to you.'

'No, Mum, I'm done talking.'

She ran out to her car, leapt in, jerked the gearstick into drive, and sped away.

Cornwall Park was busy with families and their dogs, with joggers, walkers, and tourists heading up to the top of One Tree Hill. Olivia strode out under the massive trees, her hands stuffed in her jacket pockets, her chin down. And let it all in. Everything that had shaped her. Dad abandoning her. Her mother. Zac. *Her life.*

The answers for the future were elusive. *But I want to try. I love Zac. No denying it.* So now what? Race around to his apartment and tell him the good news? Leap into his arms and hang on for dear life?

Even as she spun around to return to her car and do just that, common sense prevailed.

Am I absolutely sure?

Hurting Zac was not on the agenda. There were a lot of things to think through, and she'd take her time, spend the next few days getting her head around the fact that she could be about to change her life for ever by giving her heart to Zac. By letting go of some of the control that had kept her on track most of her life.

Scary. Downright terrifying.

* * *

The days dragged. Sleep was elusive and work tedious. Her head was full of arguments for and against getting involved with Zac. *More involved.*

I love you, Zachary Wright. But I can't have a life with you, her old self told her. *I'll hurt you.*

Every day she got texts.

Hey, isn't Josaia doing well? He's like a new kid. Hugs, Zac.

Yep, their young patient had turned into a bright and bubbly boy desperate to get out and play.

CC, you want to have dinner at that new Italian place? Zac.

Absolutely, yes. But she didn't.

You okay? I'm here for you. Hugs, Zac.

No, I'm not okay. I'm missing you. So much it's like there's a hole where my heart used to be. She thought of those shoulders she liked to lean against, that strong body that made her feel safe and warm. And missed him even more.

Did your mother go into the clinic this week? More hugs, Zac.

Yes, surprisingly, Mum had.

Olivia didn't answer any of the texts. When she found a huge bunch of irises in gold and purple paper on her doorstep on Thursday night with a note saying,

'Love, Zac,' she wanted to cry. Oh, all right, she did cry. But she didn't ring to thank him. Or to acknowledge what his message might mean.

Friday night he sent photos of his nephews. 'Check these guys out. I'm mending bridges.' The cutest little boys hung off Uncle Zac's arms, beaming directly at the camera. Zac looked happy but wary. It wasn't hard to see him with his own kids hanging off him like that. Her heart rolled. She wanted that—with Zac. Children. She had no idea how to raise kids but with Zac at her side she'd learn.

Saturday morning her phone rang. She sighed when she saw the number. 'Hello, Mum.'

'Darling, come and get me. I hate it here. They treat me like a child. I can't have anything I want.'

'Where are you ringing from?' Patients weren't allowed any contact with family for the first few weeks.

'I'm at a coffee shop around the corner from the clinic. The coffee's terrible but the owner let me use the phone. Hurry, Olivia. I can't stand the place.'

'Mum, listen to me.' It hurt to breathe. 'I am not coming to get you. You have to go back and start getting better.'

'It's him, isn't it? He's told you to do this.'

'Don't blame Zac.' *I am finally opening my eyes and seeing that to be kind to you I have to be strong and hard.* '*I* want you to stop drinking.'

'Come and get me so we can talk about it,' her mother wheedled.

'Sorry, but I've got someone to see.' Why had she left it so long? Zac was her man.

'What about me?'

'Mum, I love you, but I am about to put me first.' *Me and Zac.* 'Don't bother coming around to my house. I won't be here. Please go back to the clinic. Do this for yourself.' She cut their conversation, then turned the phone off and put it in a drawer. She was on a mission and didn't want any interruptions.

In her bedroom she gazed into the wardrobe, trying to decide what to wear. That red dress stood out amongst the dark winter clothes. Reaching for it, she hesitated. Zac had lost his mind when she'd worn it in Fiji but this was early afternoon and it was very cold outside. The many trousers and blouses were too work-like. The green skirt she pulled out didn't excite her either. In the end she slipped into the designer skin-tight jeans and silk blouse she'd worn on the day of the gala when they'd caught up again at the hotel. Zipping up the knee-high boots, she did a twirl in front of her mirror. 'Not bad.' For the first time in days she could feel some control coming back, could feel her body tightening up. The thigh-length coat from that day completed the look, and made her smile briefly.

A quick check of her make-up and a swipe of her hair with the brush and she was on her way, not giving herself time to think about what she was doing. Laying her life on the line was what this was about.

Stop thinking, just concentrate on driving through the downtown traffic.

What if—?

No what-ifs, she told herself as she pressed the buzzer for Zac's apartment. *This is do or don't. And don't is no longer an option.*

'Hello?'

It's not too late to run. 'Zac, it's me.'

A soft buzzing and she was stepping into the elevator. She didn't hesitate but pressed the button for the penthouse floor and held herself ramrod straight, ready for anything, refusing to acknowledge the flapping sensations in her stomach.

Zac was standing outside the elevator door as it opened. His smile was friendly but cautious. 'Olivia.'

'Zac.' Suddenly the full import of what she'd come to say slammed into her like an avalanche. Her hand went out to the wall to steady herself.

He took her elbow. 'Come into the apartment.'

Through the thick layers of coat and silk blouse she felt heat spreading out from where his fingers touched her, filling her with courage. Reaching behind her, he said, 'Let me take your coat.'

As she shrugged out of the sleeves she breathed deeply, boosted her courage. Then she turned to face him. 'I'm sorry I haven't been returning your texts or thanking you for the flowers.'

'That's okay.'

'But it isn't. I was rude, and there is no excuse for that. Zac, I came to tell you I love you.' There. She'd done it.

That smile didn't change; didn't fade, neither did it widen or soften. 'I was hoping you might.'

'I think I always have, but I've been so busy trying to deny it that I've made a lot of mistakes.' This was hard, yet relief was catching at her. 'Is there a future for us?'

'What do you want, Olivia? Marriage? Children and a dog?

Too much too soon. She took a step back. 'Could we try living together first? See how that goes? I didn't have good role models growing up and I'd hate to make the mistakes my parents did.'

Zac closed the gap, standing directly in front of her. He ran a finger down her cheek and over her chin. 'No, sweetheart. It's all or nothing. I love you and I want the whole picture.'

He loved her. To hear those words did funny things to her heart. Wow. To hear Zac tell her he loved her was the most wonderful thing. She smiled at him, sure her face was all goofy-looking.

Then the rest of what he'd said hit her, and she shook her head. 'I know nothing about happy families. I don't even know if I can love you and kids and my mother. I've kept myself shut off from all that, only ever loved one person.'

His mouth softened and the kiss he placed on the corner of her mouth felt lighter than a butterfly landing. 'I'll help you. But I don't want a practice run. Let's get married, jump in boots and all, a full commitment to each other and our lives. I believe in you, Olivia. If you falter *we'll* work it out. Just as I expect you to do for me. My family history isn't any more encouraging than yours and yet I want to make it work with you.'

Hope began to unfurl at the bottom of her stomach. 'Really? You want all that with *me*?'

Now he gave her the full-blown grin she enjoyed so much. 'That's only the beginning, girl. There're the hot nights in bed, the lazy days lying in front of your fire and eating takeout food, the days when we're both working so hard the only contact we have is by text, but we'll always know we're there for each other.'

'What about the days my mother does her thing?' He'd seen what she could do.

'We support her and try to turn her back on track. We do not split up over her. We will be together, in love, war, and everything in between.' Those arms she'd been hankering for wound around her waist and drew her close so his eyes looked directly into hers. 'I love you,

Olivia, more than life itself. Please, say you'll marry me.' His mouth hovered close to hers, waiting.

'Okay. Yes, please. I will. Let's get married. Sooner rather than later.' Talk about jumping in at the deep end. But somehow she didn't think she was going to drown, not with Zac holding her. 'Did I mention I love you?'

'Not often enough for me to be absolutely sure,' he said just before claiming her mouth with his.

Minutes later Zac lifted his head. 'Now I know why I had the impulse to buy a bottle of your favourite bubbles. Come on, let's celebrate.'

'Just one glass.'

'CC, relax. You are not an alcoholic.'

'No, but I want to take you to bed and have my wicked way with your body, and too many glasses of champagne might spoil the fun.'

'Can't argue with that.' Zac grinned and hooked his arm through hers. 'Come on, we've got a cork to pop. And you can tell me why it took you so long to drop by.'

'Not tonight. Tonight's for us. But I'll fill you in soon enough. Promise.'

EPILOGUE

Fourteen months later

'HAPPY WEDDING ANNIVERSARY.' Zac sank onto the edge of their bed and placed a tray with breakfast on her knees. In the corner beside the small bowl of maple syrup for the pancakes and bacon was a tiny box.

Picking it up, she locked her eyes on the man she adored and who had been everything he'd promised and more since that night she'd told him she loved him. 'What's this?'

'Only one way to find out.'

When she flipped the lid a set of exquisite emerald earrings and a matching bracelet sparkled out at her. 'They're beautiful,' she squeaked.

'For a beautiful woman. Here.' He slid the bracelet over her hand. 'Perfect.'

She put the earrings in and then reached for the top drawer of her bedside table. 'Happy anniversary to you.' She placed a small, thin box in his outstretched hand and sat back to watch his reaction.

'What's this?' He gaped at the plastic stick he held up. 'Are we—?'

'Yes, we're pregnant. And I can hardly wait.' This past year had been wonderful, and not once had she faltered. Not even when Mum had run away from the clinic twice. With Zac there she could face anything. 'We're going to be parents, great parents.'

'Yeah, sweetheart, we are.' His kiss was made in heaven and had consequences that kept them busy for most of the morning and left the pancakes to go cold and gluggy on the plate.

Her hero for sure.

* * * * *

MILLS & BOON®

Let us take you back in time with our Medieval Brides...

The Novice Bride – Carol Townend

The Dumont Bride – Terri Brisbin

The Lord's Forced Bride – Anne Herries

The Warrior's Princess Bride – Meriel Fuller

The Overlord's Bride – Margaret Moore

Templar Knight, Forbidden Bride – Lynna Banning

Order yours at
www.millsandboon.co.uk/medievalbrides

MILLS & BOON®

Why not subscribe?
Never miss a title and save money too!

Here's what's available to you if you join the exclusive **Mills & Boon® Book Club** today:

- *Titles up to a month ahead of the shops*
- *Amazing discounts*
- *Free P&P*
- *Earn Bonus Book points that can be redeemed against other titles and gifts*
- *Choose from monthly or pre-paid plans*

Still want more?
Well, if you join today, we'll even give you
50% OFF your first parcel!

So visit **www.millsandboon.co.uk/subs**
to be a part of this exclusive Book Club!

MILLS & BOON®

Why shop at millsandboon.co.uk?

Each year, thousands of romance readers find their perfect read at millsandboon.co.uk. That's because we're passionate about bringing you the very best romantic fiction. Here are some of the advantages of shopping at www.millsandboon.co.uk:

* **Get new books first**—you'll be able to buy your favourite books one month before they hit the shops

* **Get exclusive discounts**—you'll also be able to buy our specially created monthly collections, with up to 50% off the RRP

* **Find your favourite authors**—latest news, interviews and new releases for all your favourite authors and series on our website, plus ideas for what to try next

* **Join in**—once you've bought your favourite books, don't forget to register with us to rate, review and join in the discussions

Visit **www.millsandboon.co.uk** for all this and more today!